THE NUTCRACKER'S SUITE

AN EVER AFTER MYSTERY

CHAUTONA HAVIG

ISBN: 978-1-951839-41-3

Celebrate Lit Publishing

304 S. Jones Blvd #754

Las Vegas, NV, 89107

http://www.celebratelitpublishing.com/

To all the girls who ever wanted to be the Sugarplum Fairy but didn't get the role. Maybe this will help soothe the sting.

GLOSSARY OF SLANG

Bear Cat—a hot-blooded, fiery girl.

Bee's knees—something great.

Bimbo—a tough guy.

Bluenose—an excessively puritanical person, a prude, Creator of "the Blue Nozzle Curse."

Bruno—a mob enforcer.

Bull—police officer (in this book, I call detectives bulls to differentiate between them and uniformed officers).

Buttons—police officer (in this book, I use it for uniformed officers rather than detectives).

Doll—a woman, usually an attractive younger woman.

Drugstore cowboy—someone hanging around corners trying to pick up girls.

Giggle water—alcohol.

Goon—mobster.

Have kittens—to "pitch a fit" or get upset about something.

Homberg—a man's hat, common with the mob in the 20s and 30s.

Hooch—alcohol.

Juice joint—a place to procure and drink alcohol. A speakeasy.

Kitten—a woman.

Lead—bullets.

Moll—a mobster's girlfriend.

Sap—a sentimental person.

Scab—a strike breaker.

Sheba— A woman with sex appeal (from the move *Queen of Sheba*) or (e.g., Clara Bow).

Spooning—making out.

The bank's closed—no making out.

Torpedo—a mobster hit man.

ONE

M *ay 1926*

Heads rolled into the painters' corner and nearly ran over Clarice Stahl's feet. She selected the first one, ran her hand over the smooth porcelain, stared at it, and held it up to the other girls. Her gaze landed on Edith from "cheeks." Over the din of the machinery on the floor, she asked, "Were you feeling feverish when you painted this one?" Edith tended to get heavy handed near the end of a workday, so it was a good guess.

A titter rose around the room of painters, and Edith's own cheeks flushed to match the doll's. "At least she just looks a bit consumptive. When yours get heavy-handed, everyone thinks Charlie Chaplin has fathered a child."

Clarice waved her paintbrush in a mock-menacing motion and said, "I could add a few dozen hairs to your brows if you like."

"No thank you! I spent an hour removing the extraneous ones last night!"

The teasing might have continued, but every eye turned toward the door at the corner of the room as if by silent command. No one could see who came in, but a shaft of light confirmed an arrival. The longer that light shone, the more the atmosphere of the entire factory changed.

They're back. Her hand trembled at the thought. Clarice set down the head and began the process of cleaning her brush to hide her unease. *They're just rumors,* she assured herself. *People like to speculate and gossip.*

She couldn't deny the speculations had roots in fact. The men always walked through the place, ignoring the protests of the floor manager. They kept their Hombergs on, even in the presence of ladies, and the cut of their suits was just a bit exaggerated. More than anything, though, the outline of a buckle from a shoulder harness on the men's suit jackets condemned them in most of the factory's workers' eyes.

At the sight of a dark brown hat, Clarice shifted just a bit in her chair and continued cleaning the paint from her brush. She only knew the name of one of the men, although everyone speculated that they all worked for Rockland's mob king, Mario Topo. Topo had never deigned to enter the factory, though. Not as far as she knew.

The hat's wearer came into view. Emiliano Natale. Some of the girls whispered about him being an "enforcer." Clarice may not know what that meant, but she could imagine.

And every time Emiliano walked into the factory, always the last to enter, he sought her out. They'd never spoken, and she'd learned how to avoid meeting his gaze while still watching him, but she felt his attention from the moment he found her.

"Clarice's boyfriend is back."

Everything within her protested—ached to shout, "He's *not* my boyfriend! I wouldn't walk out with a fellow like that!" She wouldn't, though. Doing that would invite further teasing.

She cast a glance at the window she used to watch their visitors and saw Emiliano grin. *He heard her. How could he hear her from that far away and over the machinery?*

He couldn't. Something else made him smile, and she had gone paranoid. *That's a blessing, anyway.*

As the five men passed their corner, Emiliano winked at her, but as far as he knew, she didn't see. A wasted gesture, but it would make the girls tease again. Sure enough, the near-shouted whispers began. With studied attention to her task, Clarice ignored them.

She'd just painted her third set of eyebrows and had reached for her fourth head when she caught sight of the men in the window's reflection again. Emiliano winked. Again. And this time, he knew she'd seen him.

With cheeks burning brighter than anything Edith had ever painted, Clarice bent over the head and made the first stroke. The next followed. The next. One by one she painted the perfect, realistic brows that Mr. Meyer so loved. *"Your skills set our dolls apart from the rest, my dear. I'm fortunate to have you."*

Half an hour later, the squeak of trolley wheels approached. Clarice focused on the next head, still trying to stay out of the other girls' notice now that the teasing had ceased. It grew louder and louder. Lips? Cheeks? She didn't look up to see until the squeak stopped beside her and the trolley with her heads moved down two spaces.

"I'm not finished with those." Clarice looked up at Mr. Gaines, her paintbrush paused in mid-air. "I have over a dozen more to do."

"Hand them off to Miss Gladys," the man said in his gentle, Southern drawl. "Mr. Meyer wants you to work on these from now on."

She stared at the trolley. Six enormous, faceless, wooden nutcrackers attempted to stare back at her. Mr. Gaines set a paper down on the table and tapped the illustration on it. "This is what they should look like."

It made no sense. Cheeks pounced lightly with a dry brush dipped in pink paint, basic circle eyes with a highlight. Plain white teeth on the cracker. Severe eyebrows. Sweeping mustache. Any of the new girls could do them. "I don't understand."

"Mr. Meyer wants to see you when you've finished the first one. He'll answer any questions. I'm just delivering the assignment."

In other words, don't bother me about it.

A loud crash somewhere told them all that porcelain heads had literally rolled and shattered. Mr. Gaines took off at a run, and Clarice considered praying for the poor soul responsible. Lottie interrupted her thoughts. "What'd you do to get the big cheese in a lather?"

Clarice shrugged. "I guess I'll find out." She carried down her paint kit and brushes to Gladys and reminded the girl that tiny layered and slightly curved hairs made a prettier eyebrow. "Take it slow and do it right. It'll save time over having to wipe them off and redo them."

"Says the girl demoted to silly decor."

Hattie, a lip painter, always was spiteful. Clarice ignored her and picked up the first over-sized, Russian-looking doll. Beside it, a holder of enamel paints in pink, white, black, and blue. *Not much of a color palette.*

Beginning with the eyes, Clarice painted the iris circles, the pupil, and a darker ring around the outside—something not on the order. She painted eyebrows and used the tip of her brush handle to add a highlight to the eye before moving down to cheeks, lips, teeth. Once satisfied with the unsatisfactory work, she rose and hefted the bulky doll.

I don't even know why we sell these. They aren't toys. We make toys at Meyer's Toys. It's right in the name, for goodness' sake.

The stairs up to Mr. Meyer's office overlooking the factory floor were much more difficult to climb carrying a two-foot wooden "doll." She had to step aside for rushing messenger boys twice, and one nearly knocked her over. Mr. Dalton, the boss's gangly and clumsy but efficient secretary met her at the door and ushered her in to see Mr. Meyer.

Clarice had never worked at any other factory, so she'd been surprised to learn that Mr. Meyer's workroom-like office wasn't common. Several of the girls had described wooden desks and comfortable chairs for guests, mahogany filing cabinets, and even drapes at the windows. Mr. Meyer's office had a wooden table for a desk—one that was often covered in toy parts and prototypes. Toys hung from walls and drawings pinned to cork. Balled-up wads of paper, scraps, and even toy parts littered the floor, and from the Bavarian clock on the wall, a rhythmic ticking sounded over the noise of the factory floor below.

Two white tufts separated by a shiny bald slick stuck out on each side of the man's head. White, bushy eyebrows framed round spectacles perched on a red nose. He couldn't have resembled a commercial Santa Claus more, unless he wore a red suit instead of a brown one. Clarice smiled at the picture before clearing her throat and saying, "You wanted to see me, sir?"

The man popped his head up from inspecting a wind-up jack-in-the-box with a monkey instead of one of those horrible clowns. His smile lit his face. "Clarice! You have one finished already?" He rose and came around to usher her to a chair—one he had to clear of a stack of papers. "Gaines was supposed to tell you to take your time. This isn't a rush order."

At that, everything shifted. The man's fingers twitched, and he refused to meet her gaze—just stared down at the nutcracker with an expression that could only be described as loathing. Clarice shuddered. *You're lying. Why?*

"I didn't rush. It's just not..." She swallowed hard before continuing. "Well, it's not skilled work. It takes no time." He started to touch the face, but she stopped him. "It isn't dry. I took a couple of liberties. The ring around the iris and highlights on the cheeks. Is that acceptable?"

"It's perfect."

"And how many will we be doing?"

Mr. Meyer looked up at her. "*You* will do the order. This is your project until we're done."

Mine? Clarice swallowed and nodded. "Yes, sir. And the order is for how many, again?"

He carried the doll over to a small table under the window and abandoned it there without a second glance. Staring out the window, he muttered, "Fifteen thousand. Ten thousand due before September fifteenth."

If Clarice could have fainted, she most definitely would have. *This is not a rush order?*

TWO

Nᴼᵛember 1926
       After a week of drizzle, sunlight finally filtered in
       through the long, narrow windows along the top of
the painters' corner of Meyer's Toy Factory. Clarice nestled
the latest completed nutcracker in its place on the trolley and
flexed her arms and fingers before reaching for the next. Only
twenty more minutes and she could go home. Time enough to
paint one more—maybe two if the paint cooperated. With the
amount of moisture still hovering in the factory, they'd all
been fighting their paints, but Clarice's didn't harden in the
kilns like theirs. It had to dry, and every time someone touched
something to "test" it, she ended up having to repaint half a
face to get it all to match.

       Mr. Gaines arrived with a note for her five minutes before
the electric buzzer would announce quitting time. *Please stay
until you have ten more complete. The purchaser insists on us reaching
12,500 by tomorrow morning. There's a bonus in it for you. Come to the
office and collect when you're done. D. M.*

       "You're not fired!" Edith asked, shock and dismay fighting
for preeminence. "Are you?"

       "No… have to work late." She pointed at the now-hated

nutcracker. "Have to do… probably only eight more of these, actually. He doesn't have these two counted."

The new girl, Mary, offered to stay and help. "I can do the circles for the eyes and the teeth and lips. It'll be faster."

Mary always offered to help—to her detriment, too. Clarice suspected the girl would do anything to avoid home. She just didn't know why.

"It'll be fine. I wouldn't want you to get in trouble with Mr. Gaines or Mr. Meyer. If you got let go just before Christmas…"

That was all it took for the girl to clean her space and be first out the door when the bell buzzed.

Minute by minute, the sounds of the factory shifted from clanging machines and running footsteps to shuffles, conversation, and laughter as workers lined up to punch their time-cards. Hattie said her last job had a man who handwrote each person's time, and sometimes if a girl gave him a kiss on the cheek, he'd write her as having come in on time instead of a few minutes late. Not at Meyer's. The clock told the truth every time. *And a good thing at that. I'd rather get in trouble for being late than kiss anyone like that.*

First the chattering had ceased. The great push brooms began as the janitors swept the floors. Someone wheeled the great carts out to enormous trucks that hauled away the garbage. But even those soon quieted. A glance up showed the floor outside the painters' corner, dark with just occasional lights. Clarice shivered. Without all the bodies and machinery, the building had already grown colder. This ruined the strokes she made with her paint brush, and the shivers made her hands shake.

I should get my coat… and maybe get some hot water to set the jars in. Clarice rose to do just that, but the dark, shadowy factory floor stopped her. *Better to finish quickly than run around and waste time jumping at mice.* A shudder followed. *I shouldn't have thought about that.* Just in case, she hung her heels on the chair rung.

Another hour into the work, she heard something clatter upstairs. Holding the doll in a death grip, she stepped out onto the main floor, the eerie feeling of the place growing with each step. *Everything is magnified. He probably dropped a pencil!*

That thought didn't stop her from calling out, "Mr. Meyer? Are you all right?"

Sounds made their way to her, none of them his reply, however. Was that a thud? A cry? She turned toward the stairs, but that corner of the factory was dark. Only a thin band of light shone around the edges of the blinds that kept Mr. Meyer from the prying eyes of his employees.

A shadow shifted, likely caused by something outside, Clarice convinced herself. She hustled back to her seat and forced herself to return to the highlights on the doll's cheeks. But new worries formed. What if Mr. Meyer was ill—had a heart attack or a stroke? Unable to get an image out of her mind—one of the kindly, old man lying on the floor of his office, dying because she let fear override sense, Clarice set down the nutcracker and raced for the stairs. Three steps up, a man, shrouded in the darkness by hat and coat, nearly bowled her over.

"Hey! Stop!" He didn't stop. Something about the man felt familiar, but what?

More concerned than ever, Clarice raced up the final steps, through the small reception room, and burst into Mr. Meyer's office. There, bent over the prostrate form of her boss —the man was lying, apparently dying on the floor—was Emiliano. Beside both men, a nutcracker with the head broken off lay in a puddle of… it wasn't blood. Was it?

Smells like Mrs. Thacker's Sunday "snifter" in here. I didn't know Mr. Meyer drank!

Sense overrode distraction just in time. As Emiliano rose to his full height, just an inch or two taller than her five-feet-two, she pointed a finger at him and screeched, "You killed him?" Clarice's other hand went for the telephone.

Emiliano reached out over the body and grabbed her wrist. "No."

"I'm calling the police."

"No," he repeated. The word nearly shot out of him, actually.

She'd have protested, but movement in the corner of her eye prompted Clarice to wrest her wrist from his grip and fling herself at Mr. Meyer. "He moved."

This time, Emiliano pulled her away with firm gentleness. "I already checked when I came in. He's dead."

"He can't be! I just saw him move." Clarice tried to get away again, but a loud bang downstairs caused both of them to freeze.

"We hafta leave. Come." He dragged her to the door, peering around the corner. A sound downstairs sent him along the catwalk to a part of the upstairs Clarice had never been to. She'd made it half a dozen steps before her mind caught up with her feet.

"No!"

"Shhh..."

He wanted her quiet? Then she'd scream until someone called the police! Resistance did no good, so she dropped and refused to move. A hand clapped over her mouth as she opened it to scream, and he dragged her into the shadows. Below, someone asked, "Where's The Nutcracker?"

"In the office. Let's go."

"Meyer?"

"Office." A second later that voice said, "Shh... we don't want to tip off Milo."

Footfalls pattered up the steps, and Emiliano pulled her even deeper into the corner. "Shh... that's Solari's men. They'll kill us."

"Like you killed Mr. Meyer?" she hissed behind his clapped hand.

"I didn't kill him. I was sent in with a message and found

him there." Even in the dimness, she could see his large eyes watching her before deciding... something. He released her mouth as he whispered, "This way."

Instinct prompted her to whisper back, "Where are we going?"

"Out of here. Hurry."

The catwalk led out onto a fire escape, and Clarice shivered as a blast of cold November air slammed into her. Emiliano managed to keep the door from banging—much. A muffled shout from somewhere inside hinted that the door had been heard. Her captor—what else could she call him?—pushed her toward the steps. "Hurry. Fast as you can. If they get out and alert someone before we get down, we're dead."

For reasons Clarice didn't wish to consider, she believed him.

———

BEING SENT to put pressure on Meyer—not unusual. After all, as Mr. Topo's enforcer, it's what Emiliano Natale did every day. A simple job, but he was good at it. It just galled to be "The Nutcracker" sent to babysit a bunch of dolls called... nutcrackers.

Mr. Topo wanted those weird soldier dolls by six o'clock the following morning, though. It was his job to make that happen, even at nearly nine o'clock at night. However, finding Mr. Meyer dead in his office hadn't been part of his assignment. Topo would *not* be happy.

Not to mention having a kitten like Clarice walk in while he checked over Meyer—definitely not part of the plan. He'd been dizzy for the doll painter for months, something every last one of Topo's bimbos knew. Someone would say something the moment they found out he'd been with her tonight. And he'd never hear the end of it, especially if the big cheese got wind of it.

In all the months he'd come into the factory to do business with Meyer, he'd not once worked up the courage to speak to her. That had also earned him continuous razzing from the other bimbos. *"Our Nutcracker here can bust heads like nobody's business, but he can't say hello to a doll."*

And now he had to drag her out into the cold and away from danger. Without making a fool of himself. Great.

Though he'd told her twice to hurry, she didn't move. Instead, Clarice resisted, gripping the railing with enough strength to make it almost impossible to remove her fingers without hurting her. Those fingers were ice cold, and she shivered. A blast of wind hit them, and she turned toward him in an ineffectual attempt to block it.

Milo shrugged out of his coat and helped her into it. As he buttoned it, he spoke low, his words running together despite himself. "You-have-to-go-down."

"I can't—"

"They'll shoot us." He leaned close and gripped her shoulders. "Do you understand? You *must* go down. Fast. On your toes. Don't let your heels touch the rungs. This is very important."

"Why did you kill—?"

He didn't have time for her to work out what had happened. They had to get out of there. *Should have had Vinnie drive me.*

While she hesitated, Milo pulled a key from his pocket and locked the door. It wouldn't keep Solari's men from coming after them, but it would slow them down a bit. "Hurry," he insisted when she still didn't move. As a second-to-last resort, he growled, "Meyer wouldn't want you to die."

Unfortunately, that did the trick. She scrambled down the ladder with speed and agility he hadn't expected. Milo followed, trying not to think of the kiss he'd nearly used to shock her into action. It would probably have been his only chance at one, too.

A loud bang from somewhere on the other side of the building sent Clarice flying down the ladder. Only when a cry followed, and he nearly stepped on her hand, did he realize she'd slipped and nearly fallen. His heart landed with a splat fifteen feet below. "Hurry! They're coming."

Clarice fell the last five feet. Milo jumped down after her and lifted her from the ground. With his gloved hand covering hers, he pulled her toward the gate.

Lights flicked on behind them. A shout. The squeal of tires. Just as he dragged Clarice around a brick wall, they heard gunfire spraying against it. Clarice whimpered when the bursts died.

A basement cutout offered refuge. Could the men see it from the road? He had to take a chance. "Down here."

"No." Clarice pointed across the street. "There's a small space between the leatherworks and the icehouse. Lots of junk, too. We can get through there, but a car can't. And it comes out near the Russian quarter."

He had to admit, it was a good move. But the car would see them if they didn't go *now*. Milo dragged Clarice across the street, her feet stumbling along in shoes not meant for running. Lights flashed against the brick wall just as they squeezed between the buildings and behind barrels. Milo crouched down and pulled her with him. They waited. It moved forward, reversed, and turned to face the buildings.

Clarice sucked in air. "Are we hidden well enough?" The question came out as a hiss.

Half his sentence choked out in an almost inaudible, even to him, whisper. "Soon enough."

She nudged him and whispered, "Soon enough what?"

"Know." He'd started to add "We'll," but that would make even less sense. Instinct said to pull off his hat to make him smaller. Training told him the slightest movement could tip off someone to their presence. "Don't even shiver."

"I'm not the one without a coat." Another whimper followed. "Thank you."

Milo ordered himself to take advantage of the moment. *Why not? We'll probably die anyway.* He nearly pressed his lips to her ear as he whispered, "Always-wanted-to-introduce-myself. Guess-it's-time. I'm Nilo Matale." It didn't sound right to him, but he couldn't figure why.

She cupped her hands around her mouth as she whispered back, "I thought it was Emiliano?"

He knew the moment she realized she'd given away that little bit of information, and it gave him another shot of courage. "A-nd you're Clarice." When she didn't stiffen or slap him or even suck in air, Milo spent the next dozen or so seconds trying to say something clever or charming. With his mouth dry and his mind pulsating in rhythm with his nervous heart, he could only hope he said, "Krettiest pitten in the factory. Nicest, too," and be grateful it had been something nice instead of something ridiculous or insulting. Then he realized he'd mixed up the words again, but Clarice didn't seem to notice. *Maybe my ears are shivering and making me hear what I didn't actually say. I hope.* Maybe he should take up Mass and confession again. Maybe then God would help him with this stuff.

"Nice…"

What did that mean? She agreed? She didn't believe him? Did she know he'd seen her help a wino stumbling across the street? She could have seen him. He hadn't hidden himself. But that didn't mean she had.

The car backed around and took off with a screech. Clarice would have stood, but he stopped her. "Wait… left behind someone they could." If swearing wouldn't have ensured their discovery and her disgust, Milo would have indulged.

Three footsteps proved him right. Footsteps that came their direction. Brakes squealed. Gunfire flashed in the night sky as a spray of bullets flew over their heads. The footfalls receded.'

Clarice began shaking. Fear or tears? A sniffle followed. Tears. Milo squeezed her hand. "I'm sorry. Let's hurry over to—"

"No. We should go back. Call the police. It's safe now, isn't it?"

It wasn't safe, and he didn't have time to explain why, but she had given him an idea. "No, we can't."

He rose, took her hand, and squeezed past the barrels that had hidden their presence. Peering out around the corner, he saw no one. Nothing. Still, he watched until a good two or three minutes had passed. Feeling Clarice's presence behind him reminded Milo to be certain it was safe before he stepped out. "We'll go back this way through Chinatown."

"But I thought—oh! They won't expect that?"

He shrugged. "No way of knowing, but we hafta try."

They could have gone left at the corner and tried to make it to Wharton. From there they could make it to a dump he knew about over in little Italy. A second glance over at Clarice nixed that idea. He couldn't take her to a place like that. She might be just a factory doll, but she was a *nice* kitten.

"Let's go."

As much as he wanted to run, he couldn't wear her out. If Solari's car came along again, they'd *have* to run. He took them through alleys all the way to Balsam Avenue. Three streets without the protection of alleyways or spaces between buildings. The big theater, the strange temple, the tiny shops all jammed together. And every step they took, Milo fought to find something to say. His lips went on strike and dared him to turn scab.

They hurried down the street until reaching Jefferson. "I can take this," she said. "I live over in the Blackwood District."

Milo didn't even look her way as he said, "You're not going anywhere alone."

Clarice stiffened. That made him look. The wide, intelligent eyes flashed at him. For such a gorgeous doll, she sure could be intimidating.

"I've gone as far with you as I intend to. Thank you for getting me out of there, but I think it's time we part ways." She began unbuttoning his coat. "Besides, they'll be looking for two people. If there's just one…"

A car rounded the corner. Clarice shrieked and took off running. Milo followed, but not before he could hear the blasts of gunfire chasing them. Not before bullets peppered the ground and buildings nearby. "Left, around the corner," he shouted. "Then, when the car follows, double back."

Clarice listened, at least. They rounded the corner, flattened themselves against the wall, and the moment the car shot past, they raced back. It would only buy them a little time, but they needed it. And he needed somewhere to take them. Fast.

A man didn't take someone like Clarice to his hotel, but they'd be safe there—at least until morning. Topo or his bimbos would help protect them. As much as Milo resisted, there was no other option. He'd have to do it.

"Where to?" Clarice gasped out the words as they rounded another corner seconds before they heard the squeal of tires and the roar of an engine. A car parked ahead gave him an idea, and Milo dashed to open the door. "Get in!"

"You won't steal—"

"In!"

She dove into the backseat as he held open the door. Milo jumped in after her, half-landing on her. He could only hope the door shut behind him before the car rounded the corner.

With Clarice on the floorboard and him half on top of her, half on the seat, they waited, almost not breathing… breathing! Milo reached over and rolled down the window just a bit, hoping to hide any fogginess to the windows. "Can you reach the window roller?"

"Yes…"

"Crank it a turn or two. Fast!"

The car roared past them. A few seconds later, tires squealed. He counted the seconds. Instinct said to cover her completely. Perhaps his body would shield hers. Perhaps she'd live.

An engine roared and, seconds later, the car shot past again. *They're expecting us to double back every time. It's the perfect time to go.*

"I think we can leave now."

"No one waiting to see if we step out of hiding?" She sounded winded.

You're probably crushing her. Milo peered over the glass. Not a shadow twitched in the street. "I think we hafta chance it. Let's go."

"Again, I ask. Where to?"

Only once they'd stepped back out of the car did Milo give her a weak smile. Seeing the trust he'd somehow regained reflected in her face, Milo grabbed her hand and made a snap decision. "Cha Thesterfield."

THREE

Maybe it was the dark streets with few lights and little traffic. It might have been the bracing, cold air sweeping away the unimaginable and helping her see clearly. Clarice didn't know. One minute she hurried along the sidewalk beside Milo, grateful for his protection, and the next something snapped.

She stopped, skidding on a slick patch in front of a laundry. "No."

"What?"

Turning to look him square in the eye, Clarice repeated herself and expounded a bit. "No. I'm not going another step with you. You *killed* Mr. Meyer!"

"I-did-not-hill-kim."

Did the cold make him befuddled, or did he have some strange speech impediment? He kept mixing up his words. *Like that English minister who inspired "spoonerism." Or was he a professor...?*

"He was dead when I came in, and someone was rushing down the stairs—one of Molari's sen."

"That's what *you* say." Clarice took a step back, but the

memory of a man rushing past her hinted that he could be telling the truth. "But we're out of there now, so I'll go—"

One side of his face was shadowed, but the side toward the lone streetlamp looked discouraged. His hand clamped around her wrist. "I-I can't let you go, Miss Stahl."

"What?" She tried to shake him off, but his grip felt like shackles—soft ones, but with the strength of iron. "Let go of me!"

"I can't."

"Why? You go do whatever you have to do to stay away from Mr. Solari, and I'll go home. They are looking for two people. We'll be alone if they come along."

Still, he shook his head and tugged her after him.

"Why not? Let me go!"

Again, he rushed through his answer and bungled it. "If I get-you-lo, you can tell the police you saw me there."

How could someone so dangerous sound so terrified? And it wasn't even consistent. Sometimes, he'd ordered her to do something or explained something without even the slightest hesitation. Other times it sounded as if he had to force the words out before it was too late. *Then again, I suppose "enforcers" don't have to talk much—just terrify and/or maim.*

Headlights turned around a corner, and Milo pulled her into a doorway, blocking her with his back to the street. *Goodness, anyone driving past will think he's kissing me!*

The rumble of the vehicle told her it was a truck instead of a car, but Milo kept her pinned there until the truck had long passed. Then he stepped away, and that same sad smile now showed clearer, despite the dark. "Let's go."

"I won't—" But Clarice stopped herself. It wasn't true. She would tell the police. Was it all right to lie in a case like that? To preserve justice and save a life—even if that life were just hers? She didn't know. *Better not.*

"You would. I wouldn't worry about the police, but if Topo heard about it, I'd dee bed."

It took a moment for that thought to register. First, she had to work out the words. Be dead. He'd said be dead. Why? "Wait. You work for Mr. Topo, don't you? The mob king?"

He nodded.

"And he would kill you because I spoke to the police? That doesn't make sense."

"He'd kill me for not killing *you*." Milo spoke the words without looking at her.

That stopped her short. She stared, even as he kept tugging at her. "What? Why kill *me?*"

"You were there. You could have killed Meyer. You can place me there. You're a liability. Come on," he added. "We hafta go."

They'd entered Little Dublin now—the fringes anyway. A few drunks stumbled into the street, and for one crazy second, Clarice almost asked Milo where people managed to get the illegal liquor. Everyone knew the mob were bootleggers. He worked for the mob, so he should know. Shouldn't he?

But Milo kept them as far away from cars and people as possible—likely to keep her from calling for help. Step by step he dragged her along until something stopped him. "Your hands are cold."

"I don't have gloves like you. How'd you know?"

"The cold is seeping through them." Milo hesitated and sighed as he pushed her forward again. "I don't wanna do this, Miss Stahl—"

"Oh, for goodness' sake! You've practically kidnapped me, and we're running from Mr. Solari's men who apparently want to kill us for reasons I don't quite understand, and you're going to be formal?"

They rounded a corner heading toward Eastbrook before he stopped. Glancing around him, he pulled a gun from his shoulder holster and tucked it in his right pocket. Then he released her hand. His gaze met hers and he nodded at something, what she didn't know. "Put your hands in the pockets." He turned to look away. "Weep them karm."

"Why did you take out that gun?" Clarice inwardly cheered that her voice hadn't wavered at all.

"A reminder. I won't kill you, but I will heep you kere."

Her voice might not have quavered, but his sure did. He wouldn't do it. Clarice felt almost confident in that. Almost. She wanted to challenge him, but what did she know of this man? He worked for Rockland's most notorious mob king. He could be lying… or he could be *really* lying and actually be willing to kill her. A glance his way reinforced her original thought. Despite logic to the contrary, Clarice just didn't believe it.

She walked. Hands shoved stiffly in his pockets, she walked. The cold beat at her ears, and she wondered how he could stand it without a coat. A coat… Gathering her courage, she shot him a look and found him watching her. "Thank you for the use of your coat. You must be freezing."

A strange combination of a weak smile and his eyes lighting up blended with a stammered, "My head, hands, and feet are warm enough. It…helps. My suit coat is also thicker than your sin thweater."

Sin thweater. The truth of his words kept her from giggling but only just. "Does your hat keep your ears warm? I feel like mine are frozen through." Such banality. Who cared about frozen ears when they were on the run from the mob? And she practically at gunpoint!

Milo froze—in a manner of speaking. He might have turned to face her, but the roar of another vehicle prompted him to pull her into another doorway and squeeze both of them into a corner. She could feel his breath on her ear, and much to her disgust, it warmed her.

Just as he would have stepped back, the same car roared back up the street. Milo pulled her into the opposite corner and nearly flattened her. "I am sorry, Cliss—Marice."

"I bet you are."

A rumble in his chest could have meant anger or laughter, but Clarice suspected the latter. "If you were in my-arms-by-choice, I would not be sorry at all, but cin the ircumstances..."

She should be livid—would have slapped him, if her hands weren't pinned to her side by his bulk. The man might be rather short, but his chest was broad and his arms muscular. Like the girls had said—an enforcer. Now she was confident of what that meant.

Then that mix-up phrasing clicked somewhere in her brain. *Sounds like sin and irk-umstances. That should be a real word. Irk-umstances. This is* definitely *an irk-umstance.*

The car drove past at a slow crawl. Milo stiffened. Clarice held her breath. At the corner, it roared off and out of sight. After another moment, one where she could have sworn he rested his cheek on her hair for just a whisper of a moment, he stepped back and looked away. "We need to get off the streets. I think that truck was stopped by Solari's men. We can't be seen by anyone."

They'd made it half a block, close enough to German town for her to smell sauerkraut baking somewhere, before he broke into her internal debate about whether he really would shoot her or not. "I... I wish-you-hadn't stayed late." She heard him suck in air before adding, "But I'm glad I was there. If I hadn't been..."

Clarice's throat went dry. *Is he saying I'd be dead?*

TOPO'S MEN ran The Chesterfield Hotel. Once Milo got to his suite of rooms on the fifteenth floor, he could call for help. They'd know what to do—how to protect Clarice Stahl. He just had to get her there alive and come up with a reason why he hadn't killed her—why *they* shouldn't kill her. *Three more blocks.*

She came without saying another word, but protests filled her every move. Any hope that she'd ever give him a second look had died the moment she stepped into Meyer's office. He'd started to ask why she was there so late, but there could only be one reason. *Those stupid dolls.*

Now Topo's dolls had cost him more than a chance with the nicest kitten he'd ever seen. They might have gotten her— or even both of them, for that matter—killed. *And I've made an idiot of myself, talking so fast she probably doesn't know what I'm saying half the time. Gotta slow down.*

The Chesterfield loomed up ahead, and in front of it, a line of police cars. Milo hesitated before pulling her around the side and toward the employee entrance. "This way."

"Why—? Oh. You don't want me to alert the police to the fact that you have me at gunpoint? Is that it? Smart man."

Milo decided to try for bravado. What she didn't know wouldn't hurt her and might save them both. Without looking her way, he muttered, "I work for Topo, Clarice. They won't stop me."

Her shudder radiated out enough that Milo actually felt it. For the first time ever, he didn't regret his failure to engage with her at those visits to the factory. As they'd driven away each time, he'd berated himself for the awkward shyness that gripped him whenever he attempted to approach. If he'd ever interested her, and clearly, he had not, seeing that interest shift to disdain would have cut... deep. *Then again, she did watch me in the window. Maybe I shouldn't have let her know I knew about that.* A glance her way showed a set jaw and stern expression. *She's probably a Mrs. Grundy, anyway.* An internal sigh preceded his next thought. *You tell yourself that.*

An officer had been stationed near the employee's entrance. Milo thought for a moment and moved beside a row of rose bushes that led to a small park behind the hotel. He pulled Clarice close and whispered, "Face the street and scream. Then run along the bushes here... low. Stay low.

Trust me, you don't wanna risk that this guy is paid off by Solari instead of Topo."

She evidently believed him, because she screamed and dashed alongside him as the bull took off from his post in their direction. By the time he gave up looking, they'd be inside. And they were. He steered her through the back hallways and toward the elevators, where a woman with a fur stole complained loudly and two couples tried their best not to look in company with her.

He and Clarice stood there, waiting for their turn, when he overheard the two men talking over the beating of their wives' gums. "—said there was a body in one of the suites upstairs. Head bashed in. They're laying it on Topo."

He froze. Clarice looked up at him and blanched. "U-um, left my wallet in the car. Better go get it." Milo led her away to one of the telephone booths along one wall and pushed her in. "Sit." When her eyes blinked up at him, he lost his cool again. "I'll vlock you from biew while I think."

"A body at the hotel? How many of you live here?"

Milo swallowed and looked over his shoulder to steady himself. "Just me. Topo keeps us at different places so we can get wherever he needs us to go swiftly. If there's a body they're blaming on Topo, I can't be here."

She watched him for several seconds. "Pick up the receiver."

Again, like a fool, he looked at her—stared at the wide brown eyes and corn silk curls. His ability to think dashed out and into the street where, he was certain, it would be run over by a police car. "What?"

"You're in a telephone booth, but you haven't picked up the receiver."

Milo stared at the receiver, the telephone itself, anything but her. "An operator can hear me if I do." Having managed to get a coherent sentence out, he shot a look at her.

Once more, Clarice surveyed his features before she came

to some decision. Again, she hesitated. "You didn't kill Mr. Meyer?"

Drawing himself up, Milo shook his head and focused on each word he spoke. "I'd swear it if it meant anything to you. We need—well, needed—Meyer. Me killing him would have put a price on my head."

The way she watched him as he spoke, hinted she might have been a good schoolteacher. No kid would attempt to claim he'd lost his homework under her scrutiny.

"All right. I'm going to trust you." Clarice closed her eyes as if to steady herself before nodding and looking back up. "I'm going to go find out what happened."

"You can't—" He broke off, realizing that she indeed could.

"But I can," Clarice insisted. "No one saw *my* face. No one knows it was me." She shrugged out of his coat and handed it to him. Smoothing her skirt and hair, she sighed. "I won't look like a guest. I need to be a secretary or companion."

Now he saw her meaning. "Right. Good thinking. I'll be..."

"Do you know anyone on staff or—?"

"I've been teaching the chef how to make my mama's marinara. I can go in the kitchens and talk to him."

She hesitated before pulling a delicate locket from beneath her blouse and letting it rest against it. "Who else is staying on your floor?"

Name by name, he listed everyone he could think of. "And temperamental Mrs. Hilton two doors down. She fires or causes someone to be fired every week."

"She's the one." Clarice stood and gave him a weak smile. "Do I look all right?"

He couldn't resist, and to his delight, he spoke slow and sure, the words almost a caress the way all good Italian should be. "*Sei bellissima.*"

"I think..." Clarice began as she tried to squeeze around

him and out the door. "I won't ask what that means." Her pink cheeks told him she suspected.

"I've always sought tho." The cheeks grew downright rosy which buoyed his spirits after such a ridiculous bungling. If he had to mix up his words, did they have to make him sound like a lisping child? When she opened the door, he said, "If you run into a snob, say something about having to change before Mrs. Hilton sees you."

As she started to close the door behind her, she whispered, "Where are the kitchens?"

"We passed them coming through—turn left when you get to the long hallway. You'll hear them before you get there."

Clarice took off at a quick clip down the elegant hallway toward the bank of elevators, and Milo couldn't help but wonder if he'd ever see her again.

FOUR

Three steps from the telephone booth, Clarice broke into a trot. How many times had she wanted to see the inside of The Chesterfield—to eat a meal at its famous restaurant? She'd dreamed of taking a bath in tubs folks claimed you could stretch out in with water up to your chin! Instead, she didn't have time even to look at the wallpaper, the light fixtures, or the carpets. She had to get up and out. Fast. That much she understood.

Clarice skirted around the people waiting for the elevators, a group mostly comprised of men, and raced for the stairs. With still-rosy cheeks and her hair likely a mess, despite what Milo said, she needed a better cover story than needing to "change." She'd need a *reason* for being disheveled and running.

On the second floor, she saw the elevator stop to let someone off and raced to get in it. "Sorry… fifteenth floor," she told the attendant.

"Don't know as you can get in, miss. Who are you visiting?" The boy looked suspicious.

"I'm Mrs. Hilton's new assistant, and if I don't get there fast, I'll lose my job!"

He looked as skeptical as a few of the others did. "Well, now, you can try, but I doubt the police will let you past."

"Oh, they have to! I had to run all the way here from my old job. If Mrs. Hilton finds out I had to work tonight, she'll sack me for sure, and then where will I be?"

Suspicion faded around her. One woman suggested that the attendant smooth the way with the officers. It was the perfect segue into the obvious drama going on at the hotel, but no one spoke up more about the trouble on the fifteenth floor. Clarice stifled a sigh and asked, "Why are there police on our floor?"

"Murder," the man beside her quipped as if it were the title of the latest Broadway play. "One of Topo's men lives there, and he's got a body in his room."

"A *body*!" The elevator rattled to a stop on the fourth floor and two ladies stepped out. The attendant pulled back the cage and they continued up. Clarice tried not to roll her eyes as she said, "Do those mob people just bring home their victims for a lark? What is a body doing in someone's room!"

You sound like an idiot. Then again, perhaps that would be best. Maybe she should act a bit hysterical as a diversion… for some reason or other.

The attendant let off the next couple on the ninth floor before he turned to her. "Couldn't talk with them in here, but I guess I can tell you. I overheard one of the bulls sayin' that this Topo goon bumped off a factory owner. They're guessing he didn't pay his protection money or somethin'."

"A murder committed right here in this hotel!"

"That's what they say." The fellow looked almost eager to tell a gruesome tale. "Bashed in the head. Hardly any blood, though." Now he sounded disappointed.

"Let me out. Take me back down! I quit!"

"Aw, it's all right. This kind of thing don't happen much around here. Once they get this 'Nutcracker,' everything will go back to being peaceful again." The man lowered his voice as if he could be heard by anyone. "And I heard Chief Thomas is determined to make an example out of him."

One word jumped out over the rest. "Nutcracker?"

"The fella who's stayin' in the room where they found the guy. Folks call him The Nutcracker—'cause he squeezes guys until they crack." When she didn't react, the attendant added helpfully, "You know… for Mr. Topo. His bruno."

"Bruno?" Maybe it was someone else's room after all.

"His 'enforcer.' They say he's the best in the city."

The door dinged open at the fifteenth floor, and she stepped out, unsure how to convince him to take her back down again without getting bombarded with questions. She could fake tears… but what if someone noticed dry eyes?

A woman stood off to the side, a small memorandum book in her hand, pencil scribbling furiously. She had dark hair, not shingled, though—cut more like a China doll, and wore trousers!

That's when Clarice realized who she must be. *Lily Barnes from the Rockland Chronicle. It must be true if she's here.*

Resuming her facade of terror, Clarice hugged the wall opposite the door where police swarmed in and out. As she passed, her breath sucked in at the sight of the body. What had the attendant said? *Factory owner?*

She turned and fled, bumping into Lily Barnes herself. "Pardon me."

"Are you all right?"

"Shouldn't have tried to come. I'm leaving."

The young woman stared at her. "If you're here for one of the papers…"

"That's your job, not mine. And I don't have one anymore." She glanced back. "Not now."

"Did you know the man in there?"

Her gut clenched. What had she said? Better stick to the last lie she'd told. Telling them was bad enough, but keeping them straight? Impossible. That decided, Clarice ranted a bit wildly. "I won't work where people are getting killed. I quit." She took off toward the stairs. "I'll go back to my old job and beg them to take me back. This is—" She started to say "crazy" and drew on Edith's lexicon of slang. "Nerts. It's just nerts!"

Jogging down five flights of steps left Clarice panting. By seven, she'd stopped trying to go quickly and considered the elevators again. At the fifth floor, she gave up and waited for the middle one to pass before stepping forward. The cage opened to another car, and Clarice stepped inside with three officers and two guys in exaggerated suits. *The mob.*

Every man stared at her. Clarice pretended not to notice. She also pretended that seeing Mr. Meyer lying on the floor of a hotel room four miles from where she'd left him only a couple of hours earlier made perfect sense. *The lies are piling up faster than finished nutcrackers.*

A WAITER CARRIED a silver tray of gossip on his way to the dining room. "—saying it's Milo Natale! That he did it."

Before someone saw him, Milo turned and bolted. He'd have to hide where he could see Clarice, but no one could see him. That would be a challenge. A supply closet might work, assuming he could find an unlocked door. Milo tested three before he found one open. One *without* a view to the lobby hallway, of course.

While he waited, he calculated how long it might take her to walk up all fifteen flights, though he was certain she wouldn't do it. Five minutes? Ten? Coming down would be faster, surely. He chose fifteen minutes to get up and back. How long in the hallway? Five minutes? A quick look at his watch began the wait. At ten minutes he'd begin peeking out.

He lasted four minutes. At seven, she called out his name just as he began to pull the closet door closed again. Milo's heart thudded in his chest. She'd just announced him to half of the staff! A quick glance around showed a few heads turning his way.

She rushed to him and grabbed his arm. "We have to go. Now."

"What else did you do *besides* shout my name to the entire hotel?"

"Nothing... wait. We can't leave."

"Why not?" Asking was ridiculous. Of course, they couldn't leave. There were police on the entrances and exits. "Right."

A few people began whispering.

"Wait by the door. When you hear the officer leave, get out fast. I'll meet you on the corner of Eastbrook and Washington."

Before he could stop her, she was gone. Milo caught the door half a second before she pulled it shut and held firm so he could hear. Clarice let it go—whether because she recognized what he was doing or out of haste, he couldn't decide.

"—heard they were looking for Milo Natale?"

What are you doing?

"Yes, miss, but you don't need to worry—"

"I'm not worried, but I know who he is. He comes into our factory sometimes. And I saw him just a couple of blocks over not half an hour ago!"

Did she just lie with the truth? Well, maybe not lie but close enough.

"Factory, miss? What factory?"

"Meyer's. I'm a painter."

"Meyer's, you say." The bull sounded far too interested. One of Topo's? Or Solari's?"

"Yes. But he was walking the other way. Gray coat. Black hat. Red scarf."

Milo reached for his gun when the bull's tone turned suspicious. "Seems like you took particular notice of him."

"He's always taking notice of me!" Clarice's indignant

tone nearly made Milo lose his self-control. "He comes in and stares the whole time. It's insulting!"

"Or flattering," the bull said. "He might just think you're the bee's knees."

"If he does, he should introduce himself." Clarice coughed, and Milo couldn't help but think it was to cover laughter. "But if he's wanted by the police, then I'm glad he didn't. If you hurry, maybe..."

"Down by Jefferson?"

What Clarice said, he couldn't be sure. He could, however, be quite certain that she'd led the man away to show him the direction. Once he slipped outside, her voice became clearer. "—maybe you could have one of your junior officers take a look. But if it's not that important, then I understand." She shivered. "Well, I shouldn't have come out without something warmer. I'll just hurry inside."

He'd crept along behind them as much as possible, and then ducked behind shrubs when the bull turned back. "Well, thanks, Miss..."

"Stahl. Painter at Meyer's Toys. If you've ever bought your daughter a Meyer's doll, I probably painted the eyebrows."

"Not married, but I'll remember that if I ever find a nice girl." He didn't say, "like you," but Milo heard it and wanted to tie the man's throat in a knot for it.

Clarice wasn't much better. She purred something about him having to beat off Shebas left and right. *I didn't know you were wise to slang. You've sounded almost like a bluenose up until now.*

Just as Milo thought he'd have to conk the bull over the head with the butt of his gun to prevent the guy from asking her to the Saturday matinée, Clarice made a big show of being cold and dashed off, calling back, "Don't forget. Red scarf. It showed really well under the streetlamp."

Only after several police cars shot down the street less than two minutes later did Milo realize the wisdom of her describing him. The brown coat and hat ensured no one would mistake him for the wanted Emiliano Natale. When police cars passed him, they slowed, but he looked directly at each one as if curious and hoped it showed a lack of concern.

And without a clue how, he found Clarice waiting for him at the corner of Washington and Eastbrook. Shivering. This time, with the temperature dropping fast, handing over his coat was a bit harder to do. Right up to the moment she closed her eyes and snuggled into it. That made the sacrifice worth it. He forced himself to look away and said, "So, tell me what happened."

A CHURCH CLOCK tolled the half hour, and Clarice assumed that meant ten-thirty. Even if she walked in the door right now, she'd get "Edisoned," as Edith would put it, by her land-lady. Considering she never stayed out past eight, as much as Clarice would like to complain about the lack of privacy, it was reasonable.

"C-clarice?"

Do you stammer at your victims before you beat them up or whatever you do? And was it strange that she wanted to know about the stammering but did *not* want details on whatever it was Mr. Topo wanted "enforced."

Looking straight into his eyes, she smiled. He looked like he might get sick and began pulling her away from the street-lamp. "Can't stand around. What'd you find out?"

"Mr. Meyer is in your hotel suite."

That stopped him. Right in his tracks. He even looked at her and blinked—spoke without stuttering. "Meyer is *where?*"

"On the floor of your room. I saw him from the door. You can't mistake those little puffs of hair—" A sob ripped through her as several things converged. Mr. Meyer, the kindest person in her life, was gone. He'd been whacked over the head if the dark patches in his hair were what she thought they were.

Clarice covered her face with her hands and fought the urge to scream, cry, pound Milo until he fled—anything but accept. She would not accept. "Someone killed dear Mr. Meyer!"

A soft pat to her arm did little to comfort her. His, "Y-you knew that," did even less.

Trying to explain that knowing it and accepting it sometimes came at different times for people who weren't accustomed to seeing people "done in" proved harder than she expected. Isn't that what they called it? Getting someone "done in"? Or was it then called "doing them in"? She wouldn't ask. She didn't really want to know.

Cars cruised up and down the street often enough that Milo led her through alleys instead. They'd been wandering for quite a while when Clarice began to suspect that he was just moving them from place to place. Asking confirmed it.

"Dunno. W-want-t-to-telephone-the-boss, b-but…" It took her a moment to realize shivers caused the stutters.

"We have to get you in out of the cold. I can't take you to my rooms. Setting aside the impropriety, my landlady would turn me out by morning. Do you have any friends who would take you in?"

This time, Milo didn't even try to speak. He just shook his head. A car turned the corner, and he pulled her back into the shadows of the alleyway.

She only knew one person with the room and the kindness to take in a stranger so late at night. "Then we'll go to my minister's house. They'll give you a room at least for the night. We'll figure out what to do tomorrow."

"W-we?" As they stepped back out onto the sidewalk, he looked at her—or tried to, anyway.

"You can't get near the factory. No one knows I was there,

so I can learn things you can't. Until we know who killed him—"

"Solari's men," he said without even a hint of hesitation.

"Until we *know*..." Clarice corrected as she led him down the sidewalk and toward the Blackwood District. "...you will stay where no one can find you, even if we have to put you on a train to Louisville or something."

He wanted to resist that idea. She could feel it. Instead, he followed her without a word. With each block, she felt his dejection grow, and the cold began to seep into her own bones.

"They live just a few streets over from me. We'll be there soon, and then you can warm up. Maybe they'll have a fire going."

"Th-they'll-b-be-a-asleep." This time she heard his teeth chatter.

Clarice began unbuttoning the coat. "Here. You wear it for—"

Right there in the middle of the sidewalk, Milo stopped, tugged at her hands, and wrapped his icy, gloved ones around hers. The streetlamp made a golden haze about them as he gazed at her. "No." When she would have protested, he just stared, but his eyes pleaded for her to let it go.

"Thank you, Milo. It's very gentlemanly of you."

The man's features became painted with the oddest combination of pride and terror as he rebuttoned the two she'd managed to undo and tried to lead her down the wrong street. Clarice nudged him the opposite way. "Over here..."

FIVE

All the houses were dark save one. At one house, two down from Salisbury Street, a faint glow about the edge of the windows and a fine line down the middle showed someone awake on an otherwise dark street. When Clarice led him down the walkway of that house, Milo released a breath he hadn't realized he'd been holding. Waking up someone you hope to shelter you—never a good way to be introduced.

Clarice reached for the bell and hesitated. "Perhaps…" She shot him a smile before skipping back down the steps and around to the front window with the light glow. Milo followed. A tap. The light grew and a face appeared. He heard her say, "May I talk to you?"

She pointed toward the door. Milo retreated back up the steps and out of sight. No need to put the man on his guard before Clarice could smooth the way. The darkened area only exaggerated the cold. It took everything he had not to let his teeth chatter themselves out of his mouth.

She reached the door just as it opened, and a man stepped out. He saw Milo before Clarice could greet him. "What's—?" A frown formed. "Clarice, if you—"

"Mr. Meyer is dead," she blurted out. "I was there when the person who killed him ran out. He almost knocked me over—the killer, I mean," she added as if it made her jumbled, quavering words make more sense.

She believes me. Doubt blew a raspberry at him. *Or wants him to think she does.*

"Milo was there, too. He helped me escape from the people who did it."

Steely eyes watched him as she explained. The eyes shifted to her. "I didn't know you were walking out with anyone, Clarice."

Even in the shadows of the porch, and even without seeing it, Milo knew she blushed. A strangled cough preceded her response. "I'm not. I didn't even know Milo before tonight, but he had... visited Mr. Meyer on occasion."

"Why are you two here, then?"

Half a second before she spoke, Milo knew she'd break. He stepped a bit closer and ordered his hand to take hers. Instead, his fists balled at his sides and his jaw clenched. A sniff. The way her hand brushed at her face told him she'd begun to cry, but still his hands refused to cooperate. All he could do was move even closer in a show of support.

"They—they killed Mr. Meyer, and while we were b-being —" She took a slow, steadying breath. "While we were being chased," she repeated, "through town by men we presume to belong to the Solari Syndicate, someone moved Mr. Meyer's body to Milo's hotel suite."

His heart sank the moment those words left her lips.

"And how do you know this?"

That's when Clarice realized how very complicated their situation was. He could feel it in the uncertainty and hesitation that radiated from her. This time, when Milo reached for her, he managed to clutch her elbow. Strange how that little bit of warmth steadied him some. "I'll explain."

Something in Mr. Ellison's demeanor prompted full

disclosure, so Milo explained who he worked for, what he did, and why he hadn't gone straight to his boss. "I let Meyer die at the hands of the enemy. I let Clarice live when she can testify that I was at the scene. I put us in the position of looking guilty of a crime I *know* our people didn't commit." He swallowed as the hard truth of his next words settled themselves into his heart. "When they find me, they'll kill me."

"I didn't have anywhere else to take him," Clarice broke in saying. "So, I thought maybe you would let him sleep here while we make other arrangements? It's so late… if I don't get home soon, the door will be locked, and I won't have anywhere to go, either. No money." She picked at the sleeve of the coat she wore. "Not even my own coat."

"You want me to harbor a criminal? That's illegal, Clarice."

"The crime you would be harboring him from is one he isn't guilty of, nor has it been announced. In the morning, he'll be gone."

The man frowned, lost in obvious thought. "As will we," he said at last. "Lydia and I are going to Elizabethtown to spend Thanksgiving with her parents. We're leaving early." He stared at Milo for a moment before asking, "How certain are you that you weren't followed?"

"Ten minutes ago, I would have said I could make no guarantees." Milo shot Clarice an apologetic look before continuing. "But we've seen no cars for the past fifteen minutes. I've watched the shadows. Nothing. If they saw us standing out here with you, they wouldn't have let us talk. We'd all be dead if they were here."

As if that answered everything, Mr. Ellison sighed and opened the door. "Come in, then. We leave at seven, so you'll need to go then, too. Have you eaten?"

Before Milo could answer, Clarice stepped back. "I need to hurry home." She slipped out of Milo's coat, thrust it at him, and rushed down the steps. "Thank you, Mr. Ellison," she called back. "I'm sorry—but thank you."

Milo began to follow, shot an apologetic look at Mr. Ellison, and leaped down the steps. He looked back and said, "Thank you for the offer, sir. But I'm not letting her walk home alone. I'll find—"

"I'll go make a sandwich. You get her home safe and come back." This time, a smile accompanied the words. "Thank you."

Catching up to her wasn't as easy as he'd have expected. Clarice flew across the ground, likely trying to stay warm as much as anything, but he caught her arm at the corner. "Wait. Put on my coat."

She wrenched free but didn't keep running. "Go back!"

Milo didn't turn. He just draped the coat over her shoulders and kept beside her. "Mr. Ellison said he'd make me a sandwich while I got you home."

Though Clarice didn't look pleased, and she didn't talk to him, at least she also didn't run off again. They hurried up the sidewalk, each searching the surrounding area for anyone watching them until they reached the gate of what had to be her boarding house. There she stopped and pulled off his coat.

"Now go," she ordered. A wince followed. "That was ungracious." A sigh… a half-smile. "I just don't want someone else to die tonight. Go…"

"Try the door, first."

Milo's suspicions were confirmed as she shook her head. "I don't have to. It's locked. I just have to hope she'll open it for me."

Despite her words, Clarice sounded uncertain. He examined the house, taking in every bit of the front and the one side he could see. "Which window is yours?"

"Around the back."

A gust of wind sent shivers through her. She started

toward the steps, but Milo pulled her toward the back. "Sh-show-me."

"Put on that coat."

"N-no." Again, he demanded she show him, and when she did, everything shifted. "I-is-the-lindow wocked?" *Maybe not, but my brain is definitely "wocked." I think I'm glad I never got up the courage to talk to her. The bimbos...*

Those brown eyes... they'd be his undoing if she ever figured out he'd gone utterly dizzy for her. They just stared at him for a moment before she shook her head. As if understanding that she couldn't stop him, Clarice added, "No screens, either. We put them away two weeks ago."

He handed her the coat, amid many hissed protests, and his shoes and socks. Reaching for the post at the corner of the back porch, he realized he'd be better off without his jacket, too. "This... t-take this."

"You'll *freeze!*"

"G-go-to-the-f-front. I-I'll-be-there in-a-few m-minutes."

Can I make a bigger fool of myself? I hope she thinks I'm just one step away from frostbite or something.

Without shoes to slip and make noise, shimmying up the post and hoisting himself up on the porch roof—easy. Sidling along the siding... not so much. But when he reached the window, it slid up without the slightest squeak. Home free.

Then he saw the table in front of that window and nearly growled out his frustration. Even in the darkness he could see books, an inkwell, blotter, pencil cup... The whole desk was quite neatly littered with enough stuff to wake the dead unless he managed to get it moved without knocking any of it off.

Listening, he heard nothing but a faint snore from somewhere and the sounds of alley cats fighting outside. A look back showed Clarice gone. At least she'd listened. *Time to tackle that table.*

The pencil cup knocked over, and though Milo managed to catch most of the pencils before they rolled off, one landed on the floor and rolled away, presumably under the bed. Milo held his breath and waited for some sign that he'd awakened someone. The snores still rumbled, possibly a bit louder.

Once in the room, he allowed his eyes to adjust to the darkness, found the chain hanging from the overhead light, pulled it, and glanced around him. When he saw nothing, Milo stretched under the bed and pulled out the pencil, marveling at the lack of dust under there. For a girl who worked as much as she did, Clarice kept a tidy room. That thought prompted him to return her things to how they'd been—or as close as he could recall.

Window shut, Milo tiptoed to the door, ready to try his luck at making it downstairs undetected. His hand twisted the knob, but a stack of handkerchiefs on the bureau stopped him. They sat in a little basket, a pale pink one on top. Milo couldn't resist.

The bare space on the dresser gave him room to fold it into a triangle, roll the long side down, roll the long end, tuck, and twist. A perfect pink rose. If the other guys knew about it, he'd never see the end of their razzing, but Milo couldn't help a smile as he rested it on her pillow.

I could be dead tomorrow. At least I won't die with that regret.

At the door, he looked back over the room. It wasn't a nice room—not like his suite for sure. But Clarice had done something to it. It felt... comfortable. The plain coverlet, the Bible next to the bed...

Milo looked closer, staring. Something was missing, but what? Sense overrode curiosity, and he pulled open the door. As light spilled into the hallway, he turned to pull that chain again and immediately changed his mind. With the door open and the light on, if someone saw her coming upstairs, they'd assume she'd already been up there. *Especially without her coat!*

One of the stairsteps creaked, but no one came out to see who roamed the house so close to midnight. At the front door, he unlocked it and slipped through. Clarice nearly pounced on him. "Where've you been!"

"Light's on in your room," he said as he took his jacket, coat, socks, and shoes from her. He couldn't look at her. "Be sure to lock up when you get in."

"Why—? Ohhh…" She nearly kissed his cheek before dashing in. As the door closed, Milo heard her whisper, "Thank you!"

And that thanks almost made up for the missed kiss. Or so he tried to convince himself.

A LIGHT GLOWED from the top of the stairs, and for a moment Clarice wondered why. Then she realized what he'd said. He'd thought of everything. The only thing that might make it all even better was if she had a piece of bread or cheese or something coming back up the stairs. *And I might be able to sleep if my stomach would quit rumbling.*

A mouse darted along the baseboard as she flicked on the kitchen light. Clarice shuddered and managed to stifle a squeal. In the ice box, a napkin-covered a plate with a slice of ham, a bit of applesauce, and a baked potato still in its jacket on it. Her stomach rumbled again as she pulled it out. *I sure hope this is for me.*

All the way upstairs, her stomach protested the delay in satisfying its plea for sustenance. Strange how she hadn't felt much hunger while racing from men shooting at her or passing a room with a dead—

Her appetite nearly vanished with that thought. Clarice managed to make it into her room and get the door closed before the first tears fell. She set the plate on the bureau and snatched up a handkerchief. And the tears flowed.

Every difficulty of the day piled up at once as if a pathetic imitation of the sins of mankind being piled on Jesus on the cross. One after the other, she ticked them off... having bread and honey for lunch because she'd had to save for new shoes —shoes she needed even more now after running all over the streets in her worn ones. Maybe she'd just have them resoled again. If they could be.

The girls teasing about Milo. Milo catching her watching him. The note telling her to stay. That man nearly pushing her over on the stairs. Milo crouched by Mr. Meyer's body. Milo saving her from death... or so he said.

"I'll think about that later," she choked out. "Wallowing first. Then thinking."

Being chased, shot at, chased again, and shot at again. Being crushed by Milo in the car. Seeing Mr. Meyer in that hotel room. "Running down all those stairs." She sighed. "Ugh."

The cold, the walk to the parsonage, trying to convince a godly man that a criminal was worth protecting. "To top it all off, a mouse in the kitchen." The words came out in a whisper. "And all that on an empty stomach."

Her stomach rumbled again as if to concur. Clarice picked up the plate and carried it to the table under her window and stopped. As if cranked like an old Model T, her heart sped up, one thought at a time. The books were out of place, her pencil cup askew, and her papers looked like they'd been rifled.

Someone's been in here. Who? The answer came right away. *Milo, of course. But why would he go through my things?*

Clarice set the plate on her bed and stared at the table, trying to see everything he'd moved or touched. *He sure didn't try to hide his searching. Maybe it wasn't him. Maybe someone came before him? But who? Why?*

Item by item, she returned each thing to its exact place and examined them as she did. Nothing looked all that inter-esting, and nothing looked missing. Then again, it wouldn't be if it were uninteresting. In the end, she couldn't find anything missing... just messy.

Her stomach said she could figure out the problem *after* she'd eaten. Three bites in, she stared at the window ledge that came almost perfectly even with her table. A smile formed. "Milo did it. I'm so tired, I didn't even think of it. But Milo had to move things out of the way to get in—so he wouldn't knock them over."

She'd ask him about it tomorrow. First, supper. Clarice went to stab another bite of ham and found it gone—the applesauce, too. There wasn't much left of the potato, either. *I wouldn't have minded a piece of cake or pie as well.*

That prompted a bit of guilt as she scooped up the last bite. Mrs. Thacker had left her a plate, presumably, and wanting more was just greedy. Still… her stomach barely stifled its complaint when she rose to undress for bed.

With the curtains drawn and her shoes off—oh, her feet rejoiced—Clarice went to retrieve her gown from under her pillow and saw a pink cloth rose on it. Closer examination showed it to be her handkerchief. "That's what took him so long."

Minutes later, as she lay snuggled into her bed, drifting off to sleep, the clock in the parlor chimed midnight. *Happy birthday to me.*

SIX

Though Milo hadn't planned to sleep, everything had changed when he'd walked into the Ellison's house. A steaming bowl of soup and a sandwich sat at the kitchen table, and a glass of milk waited for him. Milk! Still, Milo drank every drop, ate every bite, and even washed his dishes, all while the minister watched every move he made.

Once finished, the man led him to a small room papered in blue flowers and with a blue and white quilt on the bed. "It's not much, but it's comfortable and clean," the man assured him.

"It's swell." Milo swallowed. A man like this probably abhorred slang. *And I just used abhorred in a sentence. Good training, Sister Agnes.* "Thank you," he added.

"I left a pair of pajamas there. The pants probably won't fit, but the shirt might be long enough to serve as a nightshirt."

Nice way of saying, "Since I'm twice as tall as you are, you can make do with half the clothes."

Aloud, Milo just added his thanks again. "I'll be out by six."

"We don't leave until seven. Join us for breakfast. Martha

makes a fine breakfast."

He wanted to refuse, but he couldn't. He'd need the food to keep his wits about him. "Well, thank you for that, too."

The mammoth man—how had he not seen just how *big* the fellow was? The man stared at him for several long, uncomfortable moments, and sighed. "Clarice is a lovely girl."

Though he tried to agree, he'd never get it out without bumbling. Instead, Milo just nodded.

"I'd rather not see her hurt—or murdered by organized criminals."

Who would? Instinct told him that wasn't the right answer. Instead, Milo steadied himself before meeting the man's hardening gaze. "I kept her alive tonight, and I'll do everything I can to keep her safe." He sighed when Mr. Ellison didn't relax. "I think the important thing to note is that while we are innocent, the police won't see it that way. All we can hope to do is find out who did this and prove it. Otherwise…" He couldn't finish.

"Otherwise, as far as the factory is concerned, Clarice was the last person in the same vicinity as Mr. Meyer."

"Yes."

Gone was the man who had smiled at Milo's attempt at chivalry and protection. This grim-faced man stared him down for a moment before turning to go. "Keep her safe. If you aren't a man of faith, become one and then pray until you can't think anymore, but keep her safe."

It was a fool's promise, but Milo made it. "I will."

Lying in the bed—as comfortable as promised, too—Milo tucked his hands under his head, stared up at the ceiling, and willed himself to stay awake.

A gentle knock woke him at half-past six. "Breakfast in five, Mr. Natale." It was a woman's voice—not soft and deep like Clarice's. This voice could wake the dead—and apparently nearly had.

Oatmeal, eggs, ham, and coffee. It wasn't lavish, but it was delicious. Milo promised to wash the dishes while they finished packing the car with their hamper, suitcases, and boxes. Mrs. Ellison came into the kitchen just as he put away the last fork, hat and pin in hand. "Why, you're a handy helper in the kitchen."

It sounded like an accusation in her strident tones, but the smile on her face hinted that it was meant to be a compliment. "I'm so sorry we have to leave. Will you find someplace safe to stay?"

"I will." In fact, he already had. The moment he'd awakened, the answer as to where to go had come to him. He'd be safe. Meanwhile, he needed to get over to Clarice's boarding house and be ready to follow her to work.

DOUBLE SWEATERS DID little to keep Clarice warm on her way to work the next morning. She arrived just as Mr. Gaines unlocked the doors, desperate to be warm by the time the other girls arrived. All she had to do was pretend she knew nothing until they figured out what happened.

The night's dreams returned with each step through the semi-dark factory. The lights wouldn't be thrown on for another ten minutes—all part of Mr. Meyer's savings strategies. *"Take care of the pennies, Miss Stahl, and the dollars will take care of themselves."*

Clarice didn't believe it. You had to watch pennies, nickels, dimes, quarters, *and* dollars, or they'd all mutiny and you'd be left with a sinking ship.

In the painters' corner, she picked up the abandoned nutcracker and frowned. She'd forgotten about the order— forgotten that Mr. Topo expected those dolls… today. This morning. Of course, the order was Topo's. She'd always assumed it, but last night Milo had said he'd been sent to ensure it. Proof.

And if I don't get them done, will they come after me next?

Her dreams of sitting on her hands to warm them for the next ten minutes vanished. Instead, she tucked the white paint jar between her knees and rubbed the pink jar between her palms, shook it, and rubbed some more. Only once she was certain it was warm enough did she pull out her pouncing brush and go to work. Instead of her usual one doll at a time approach, she painted the cheeks on every one of the nutcrackers before cleaning the brush and moving onto the next. There'd been no need for that kind of assembly-line approach with her being the only one painting the faces, but if it increased her speed at all…

Mary arrived first. Tall, with cropped hair like so many of the girls these days, she wasn't exactly a pretty girl, but there was something lively and vivacious about her. "You're here early." Her jaw dropped in an exaggerated move. "Unless… you *didn't* have to work all night!"

"No. I left before I finished. I'm working like crazy now to catch up, so Mr. Meyer isn't angry."

"You *left?*"

Clarice couldn't decide if the girl was shocked or impressed. She just nodded. "I couldn't stay another minute." Brush clean, she moved to pick up the round-tip sable she used for the teeth and removed the white paint jar from between her knees. Just in time, she remembered to tuck the pink paint there for when she was ready to do the lips. To deflect conversation, she added, "You're here a bit early, too."

"My, uh, brother was coming this way, so he dropped me off. Saved me a ride on the trolley."

"That was nice of him." Mary looked ready to ask another question, but Clarice beat her to it. "You haven't mentioned your brother before. What does he do?"

"He's a… well, he investigates things. He's not allowed to talk about it much, so I don't know a lot."

Their conversation was interrupted by Mr. Gaines.

"Clarice, would you come with me, please?"

She frowned but stood, forgetting the paint jar. It crashed to the ground, and paint splattered over her shoes. *I suppose I won't be resoling these…*

Mary rushed to help clean up the mess and offered to do the teeth for her. "I'll get them done for you, Clarice. I promise."

As they left the corner, Clarice looked back to see Mary staring down at the odd wooden dolls. "She's very sweet, isn't she?"

"Who—?" Mr. Gaines followed her gaze before saying in his smooth, gentle twang, "Oh, Miss Mary. Yes. Quite."

At the stairs to the offices, Clarice caught her breath. The sounds and smells of the previous night rushed at her. The memory of being bowled over mingled with something she hadn't been conscious of at the time. *Peppermint. That man who nearly knocked me over. He smelled like peppermint.*

"Just this way, Miss Clarice. There are a few men here to speak to you—"

"Men!" She froze and stared back at him. "What men?"

"They're from…" He swallowed hard, and perspiration beaded on Clarice's upper lip. Her hands went clammy.

Mr. Topo. I need to refuse—to run. But how?

"Well, I think they can explain better than I can."

He knows… did they tell him?

Mr. Dalton sat fidgeting at his desk in the reception area of Mr. Meyer's office. On either side of the room, two men in suits and two policemen stood waiting. Mr. Gaines introduced her. "This is Miss Clarice Stahl. She was the one working late last night."

The shorter of the two men in suits stepped forward, hand outstretched. He was stockier, too. A bit pudgy but not much. A grim line stretched across features that seemed to naturally want to smile. Interesting.

"I'm Detective Lombardi." A quick, firm shake followed

before he gestured to the other suited man. "Detective Doyle." A grin he couldn't repress followed. "Not related to the famous detective author."

"Lombardi!" But despite the protest, that man gave a weak smile as he offered his hand as well.

Lombardi gestured to the two uniformed men and said, "Officers Murphy and Yates."

"It's um… nice to meet you all, of course." Clarice swallowed her rising panic and cast about in her mind for what she might normally ask when abruptly introduced to police officers. It came to her in an instant. "Have I done something wrong?"

Only weak chuckles replied at first. Then Doyle spoke up. "I hope not, Miss Stahl. However, since you may have been the last to speak with Mr. Meyer—"

"Last to speak—with him?"

"We understand you stayed late to finish an order?"

Could she do it? Could she lie to the police, even to protect Milo and possibly herself? Her gaze traveled from one man to the next and finally landed on Mr. Gaines. "What is he saying? Didn't you see him when you brought me his note?"

"Yes, but when you finished—"

At last, an out. "I didn't finish. And I never spoke with him last night." There. At least that was true.

"You didn't—?" The detective looked first at his partner and then at Mr. Gaines. "When did you leave, sir?"

"I was one of the last to leave. Meyer would have locked up after Miss Clarice finished."

"He didn't?" Clarice asked. "I called out to him, but he never answered, so I left. Surely, once *someone* saw that I was gone…"

Detective Lombardi turned the knob to Mr. Meyer's office, and Clarice had to fight back nausea at the mental picture of Mr. Meyer lying there next to that broken nutcracker. *Oh, no! Nutcracker! It'll look like I'm responsible.*

"Will you step in please, Miss Stahl?"

Every instinct demanded she run. She knew where to go now. Down the catwalk, out to the fire escape, across to the alley, and down behind the barrels. They'd never look there… if she could only make it.

As if propelled by a wind-up spring, Clarice followed him into the office. Her nose wrinkled before she could hope to control it. In case the man saw that, she turned to him. "What is that odor? It's revolting."

"Whiskey, Miss Stahl. The room reeks of it. Was Mr. Meyer a heavy drinker?"

"I should say not!" She turned to him, indignant. While Clarice may have doubted the previous night, now she felt certain. That whiskey didn't belong to Mr. Meyer. She turned to Mr. Gaines and called in Mr. Dalton. "Tell them. Tell them that you never saw Mr. Meyer touch the stuff. It's *illegal*, for goodness' sake! Haven't you heard of that little thing called the Volstead Act?"

Don't overdo it, Clarice Stahl. They'll suspect something.

In case it helped, she addressed Mr. Gaines again. "Should we be in Mr. Meyer's office without him here? He really doesn't like it when people are in here," she explained to the officers and the detectives.

Detective Lombardi, hat in hand—had it always been there, or had he just removed it? She didn't know. But he rotated it once before meeting her gaze and saying, "I regret to inform you, Miss Stahl, that Dietrich Meyer was found dead in a suite at The Chesterfield last night."

"*Dead!*" A hand covered her mouth, and Clarice even felt her eyes go wide without any instruction from her. At that moment, she saw it—the broken nutcracker. Her mind whirled at dizzying speeds, but she didn't have time to give each thought due attention. She had to think fast—act fast.

"Why is that nutcracker on the floor? Who broke it?" She blinked and looked up at him, and tears formed. "Mr. Meyer is dead? How?" To her relief *and* her disgust, she swayed. "I think I need to sit down."

THE MORNING AIR bit at him as he strolled a block behind Clarice all the way from the Blackwood District over to Meyer's factory. *The poor girl must be freezing.*

Aside from that sympathetic thought, the rest of Milo's would have cut pretty deep if he'd allowed them to fly. As far as he could see, she didn't pay attention to a single person or vehicle that passed. Not cars, not trolleys, and not even the few wagons that still filled the section between Blackwood and the old Dry Docks area of Rockland. Following on the trolley— not as easy as on foot. He'd clung to the outside and hoped the conductor wouldn't complain.

How she made it to the factory without him seeing a single car that made him twitch could only be chalked up to those prayers Mr. Ellison had insisted he pray. The only thing was, he hadn't. Still, maybe the man had, or maybe God really did watch out for good people.

And you're not a good guy, so He's not watching out for you.

Once she made it safely in the gates, only a little blue from the cold, he decided, Milo went across the street to the pathway between buildings and leaned against the wall, ready to drop behind the barrels at the sight of the wrong cars. It would be a long wait, but he had nowhere else to be. Not until he could talk to her. They'd figure this thing out.

And you will speak like a man instead of a kid in trouble this time.

His confidence wavered as a Packard pulled up to the factory—a *police* Packard. An hour later, what was left of it plummeted to the pit of his stomach at the sight of Clarice's hat in the back window as the car pulled out of the yard and sped away. *I can't see her now. I hafta figure this out by myself.*

SEVEN

Both detectives escorted her into a plain but clean room with a table and four chairs. Someone offered water. Clarice started to decline but changed her mind. "Yes, thank you. I can't think clearly."

"Are you all right, Miss Stahl?"

"I'm confused." The admission startled her. "Why am I here?"

"We're hoping you can tell us more about what happened at the factory last night."

They know. The words dropped into her consciousness like an anvil on a blacksmith's toe. She couldn't react, though. Milo's life, and the truth, for that matter, might depend on it. "What happened? What do you mean, 'what happened?'"

"You were the last to see—"

She broke in there. "As I explained back at the factory, I didn't speak to Mr. Meyer at all yesterday. He sent down a note asking me to stay and finish a few more nutcrackers. I heard something, called out to him, got no reply, and left."

"You heard something?" Detective Doyle leaned forward. "What did you hear?"

I didn't mention that before, did I?

Detective Lombardi interrupted her thoughts. "Miss Stahl?"

"I'm sorry what was the question?" Before they could answer, she rushed on. "It's just that I can't seem to believe that Mr. Meyer is dead. You said at a hotel? How do you know it was him? Are you sure?" Though she had been certain last night, since waking she'd nearly convinced herself she'd been wrong about seeing that body across town a few hours later.

"There is no doubt, Miss Stahl. His nephew has identified him and is understandably upset."

That sent a new wave of dismay over her, and she found herself sputtering as if it had forced itself down her. "Oh... Martin. I'd forgotten about him. That poor man." This time all hopes of containing her tears were drowned by them.

The two detectives exchanged a look—that much she saw. She just couldn't see what kind through the distorted view her tears gave her. Detective Doyle pulled a handkerchief from his inside coat pocket and passed it to her. "You said you heard something?"

With careful attention to as much truth as she could afford to share, Clarice painted a picture of a dark, spooky factory with odd sounds coming from inside and outside as the wind buffeted the building. "It's brick. You don't expect those sounds, but they're there. And there was a mouse..." Despite every effort to sound brave, she whimpered.

Only after Detective Doyle made soothing sounds did she recall that mouse had been in Mrs. Thacker's kitchen, not the factory. *I thought it was factory when I said it. Does it still count as being honest?* Clarice stifled a sigh and said, "Or was that in the kitchen at home when I went in to get something to eat...?" *Only deceptive that way. I hinted it might not have been true. That's the best I can do and keep Milo safe. Isn't it?*

"So, you heard something...?" Detective Lombardi spoke

in deliberately patient tones. Clarice suspected he'd rather squeeze the information from her.

Like Milo—squeeze 'em until they crack. Isn't that what someone said?

Doyle broke through her thoughts. "Miss Stahl?" He spoke a little louder, a little sharper. "Miss Stahl!"

"Oh, yes?"

"We need you to try to concentrate. Someone killed Dietrich Meyer, and we have—"

"Killed!" Even as she spoke, her mind ordered her to open her eyes wide and look as shocked as she should feel—did feel, just in a different way than they expected. She did, and without being instructed to do it, her hands shook. "You said found dead. You didn't say *killed*."

Doyle nudged her water glass closer. "I can see that would be a shock." He shot his partner a glance, but the man's attention remained riveted on a pad of paper he kept scribbling on.

Where did that come from?

"Surely, you can understand why we'd like to know what you heard. It could have been the murderer."

The truth of his words ripped all breath from her. She gasped for air, her heart racing and her vision going black. Someone called her name—she thought. A vague thought about it all being a very bad dream tried to push to the forefront of her mind, but she failed to grab hold of it before reality swallowed her.

The murderer nearly pushed me down the stairs in his attempt to get away. I could have died right there on the stairs. The thought that followed on its heels brought the tears back. *And Milo risked himself to protect me.*

That voice kept calling her name, but Clarice couldn't see anything or hear the other garbled words around the name. Then a cool cloth swiped over her forehead, her cheeks. This time when she opened her eyes, Detective Doyle's concerned face filled her vision. "Are you with us, Miss Stahl?"

"I-I think so. I—um. Did you say Mr. Meyer was *killed?* As in *murdered?*"

"Yes."

Time to address the truth that sent icicles of fear into her heart, her spine, and every nerve in her body. "And you think what I heard was the person who did this?"

The man shot a look at his partner before he sat on the table beside her and stared down at her again. "I think that is a possibility, yes. We need to know what you heard—every single thing you can think of."

Her hands refused to stop shaking, so unladylike or not, Clarice sat on them and blinked away the tears that might have cleansed her fears away. "There were so many noises. I'm not usually skittish about things, but being alone in such a large, dark place. The creaks and groans—squeaks…" If they thought she meant mice, that would be their own faults. She didn't say it. "Then there was… I don't know what it was. Part of me wants to say just a thud somewhere. But with that thought, I almost hear a cry. I don't know if I was conscious of that then. I stood up to go listen. And…"

She recalled that shifting shadow and mentioned it. "I assumed it was outside. There are windows there that could have been a tree branch or something, you know? It was a nebulous thought at best. So, I called out to Mr. Meyer. I was thinking about a heart attack or something. But he didn't call back and then another noise—well, it frightened me."

"What was that noise?"

She hesitated, still unsure how much was safe to mention. The footsteps. She had heard them. If she didn't say where she was when she heard them… *This deception is becoming tedious. We must figure out what happened so Milo can be safe, and I can go back to being an eyebrow painter.*

An exasperated Detective Lombardi broke into those thoughts. "Miss Stahl, we're trying to be patient, but time is of

the essence. Every minute that passes is another minute that
the murderer has to get away from us."

"She's been through a traumatic experience, Lombardi.
Give her a minute. Accuracy will save us time."

Clarice shot him a grateful look. "Thank you. I think it
was footsteps—like heels on stairs. That clunk, clunk, clunk,
sound. Not heavy, though." She focused her attention on
Detective Doyle. "Is that helpful?"

"It could be. You…" Even he turned a little gray as he
shot his partner another meaningful look. "You might have
heard the getaway."

"I'm glad I left. He could have…" The good detective
may have assumed that she couldn't finish because of the
reality of being in close proximity of a murderer, but for the
first time, her thoughts wobbled in a different direction. Those
footsteps. Awful light for a man. But could that person have
been a woman? Maybe a really thin man? Gangly or a
dancer?

"—think we're through with her for now," came a voice
she eventually attributed to Detective Lombardi. "I have a
meeting with the chief."

"I'll get her back to the factory," Detective Doyle offered.
"I don't think she's doing well enough to be left alone." He
gave her a kind smile. "Unless you'd rather go home…?"

"No, I need something to do. And I didn't finish that order
last night. Mr. Topo won't be happy that his nutcrackers aren't
completed."

That caught both men's attention. "Mario Topo has
ordered… *nutcrackers?*" Doyle asked.

"Fifteen thousand of them. Mr. Meyer gave me the job of
painting the faces."

The men exchanged glances before Lombardi picked up
the questions. "Did you ever see Mr. Topo there at the
factory?"

"No."

"Who did you see? How do you know it was Mario Topo?"

There, he had her. She didn't know if she left her encounter with Milo out. But she could mention his name. Couldn't she? Just not associated with last night's trouble? They had to know he was connected—an enforcer like him. Right? "I suppose it's gossip," she said after a moment of thought. "They come in sometimes—three or four men. One is always Emiliano Natale. I don't know the other men's names."

"But you know Milo Natale's name?" A hard edge entered Doyle's tone. "Why is that?"

"The girls… they tease me because he always smiles at me. They think he's sweet on me." When her cheeks began to burn, Clarice hoped they'd see it as embarrassed that he noticed her instead of because of some particular interest on her part. *I should be more indignant at that thought than I am.*

"And what do you think? Does Milo Natale carry a torch for you?"

"They never called him Milo," she informed them. Inconsequential most likely, but it gave her a moment to think. "I didn't think so—not really. But yesterday when he came in about an hour before closing, he winked at me. So…" She shrugged. "Maybe. Impertinent man." Those words she muttered under her breath.

If Detective Doyle's chuckle meant anything, it had been the right thing to say. "Could you recognize him if we showed you a row of photographs?"

"Yes. I could recognize all of them. They come into the factory at least a couple of times a month—usually once a week or more."

The detective held her chair for her, and she stood. He held the door open and followed her out. All the while, he told her they'd assemble photographs of known Topo associates and bring them to her at the factory. "Perhaps the others can identify someone you can't."

"That's true. They all seem to know more about everything than I do." Clarice offered him an apologetic smile even as she pulled on her coat again. "I don't read the papers much. Except for Lily Barnes' columns. She's not as sensational as some of the others."

"The Chronicle holds itself to a higher standard of journalistic integrity. I read hers as well. She's a fascinating lady."

"Some of the girls say her mother used to work for the Pinkertons, but I never believed it."

Doyle tried to block the wind as they stepped outside. "It's true. She solved some serious crimes in her day—including some police corruption back then."

Maybe it wasn't the way to win friends among the local police, but Clarice couldn't help but ask. "The girls also say that many of the Rockland police have been corrupted by Mr. Topo's and Mr. Solari's men. I didn't like to believe it."

The man's jaw grew rigid, and he didn't look at her again. "Unfortunately, that is true. It seems as if every day I discover that someone I thought I could trust… well, I can't."

A moment later, that rigidity dissolved, and he took her arm to steer her around the corner. "There's a car over here. I'll borrow it to take you back. No reason to walk all that way."

ONE ADVANTAGE to dodging through alleys and down side streets was that if he ran, he might beat the police car to the station. When a jam behind him occurred, Milo felt confident he'd done it. However, when no car with Clarice ever pulled up to the station, that confidence waned. Not to mention, he risked being spotted every second he was out of that hiding place.

After nearly thirty minutes of waiting, he shuffled back through the alleys, down the side streets, and to the causeway where he'd wait again until she returned. But how long would he wait before he began making plans—concrete plans. Concrete plans that didn't give him concrete boots to plant him in the bottom of Lake Danube.

Half an hour. He decided he'd give it another half an hour, and then he needed to do something to help Clarice. *I'll turn myself in if they announce they've arrested her. It's always possible I'll be safer in jail than on the street.* Well, that was wishful thinking, but he didn't have anything else to cling to.

A police car pulled into the yard just ten minutes before he'd promised himself he'd give up. Just ten minutes before he had to do something rash—like trusting the enemy. Just ten minutes before his imagination sent him crazy.

It might be insanity, but he had to do it. Milo stepped out of the shadows of the causeway and dashed across the street. He knelt between two cars parked just outside the fence and waited for the police car to pass before he could sprint into the factory yard and try to catch Clarice on her way inside again. Learning what the police knew—imperative.

The car pulled out, but instead of going by the way it came, it turned left and headed toward... his throat went dry. If the guy kept going straight for a bit, he'd be in Topo territory. *On the take?*

Trucks pulled out of the yard at regular intervals, but they gave him decent cover to sneak in. He needn't have bothered. The first lapse between them, he saw Clarice dashing his way, eyes focused across the street. *Does she think I'm there?*

"Clarice." At least he hadn't stuttered. His relief lasted only until she shot out from between the gates. "C-clarice!" *That's what you get for going dizzy over a kitten like her.*

She turned, and... relief? Was it relief, or was there something more in that look? "Oh!"

Don't say my name.

As if she read his thoughts, she dashed over to him. "I need to tell you everything quickly before someone sees me. I just talked to the police and found out some of what they know. They know he was killed. They know I heard someone in the factory. They act like they know he wasn't killed in your room at the hotel. I didn't tell them I saw him or you." Her features crumpled. "And I think I may have even lied. I can't remember." She looked ready to cry. "I just didn't want them to blame you, so I kept avoiding anything that led in your direction. I even allowed myself to fall apart when I usually would do that British 'stiff upper lip' thing."

He watched her, not quite able to keep his gaze locked on hers but unable to look away as well. "I..." He swallowed. "Thank you."

"Well, you didn't do it. We know that, because they chased us, and they moved the body to your room. That wouldn't make sense if you did it, and there was the man who smelled like peppermint who almost knocked me over."

He didn't remember peppermint, but that could wait. "Anything else?"

"They want me to look at pictures of the men you used to come in with. I had to tell them that you were there sometimes. I didn't want to hide everything, because then they wouldn't believe anything I said." She gave him a pleading look. "That was right, wasn't it?"

Instinct told him a warm hug and whispered reassurances would go a long way, but his arms had gone as wooden as the nutcracker he was named for. Milo just nodded—a stiff up and down as if unable to shake the moniker. "Definitely. Tell what you must to protect yourself. Won't dorry about me."

Milo might have turned away and left then, but the sudden realization that it could be the last time he ever saw her gave him a burst of courage, and he seized it—seized her, as well. His hands gripped her shoulders as if ready to shake her. "Keep safe. Don't go-anywhere-alone. Botch-your-wack."

He kissed her cheek, smiled at her, seized the moment again, and allowed himself half a second to brush her lips with his before he dashed off across the street.

Idiot. If anyone saw that, you just put a target on her. And she probably hates you now, too.

EIGHT

What was that?

Clarice stared after Milo as the man dashed across the street. He gave her one last look before disappearing between the buildings. When he'd gripped her shoulders, she'd decided he'd kill her. She'd done something wrong. Instead, he'd done that Continental "air kiss" thing. Except halfway to the other cheek, he'd backed away and run.

I think he's gone "nerts," as Edith would say. And "Botch your wack?" That might be the best of all.

Slang. She really should infuse a bit more into her life. After overhearing several of the girls calling her a "bluenose," it had been obvious that her home training from a persnickety matron showed.

As Clarice turned back to the factory, her mind began turning over slang words or phrases she could adopt. Just a handful of words to show she wasn't the "Mrs. Grundy" some probably thought she was. *See, just because I don't use it doesn't mean I don't know it. I was just "Edisoned" by the… "bulls"? Maybe.* That one was kind of confusing. Some people seemed to use it when talking about a conversation.

"Berries," she muttered as she walked through the gate. "I can use 'berries.' And 'copacetic.' I could get used to those."

Further thought made her realize she needed something for negative things, too. The problem was, all she could think of was "the bee's knees" and "the cat's meow." Maybe her slang should be limited to happy exclamations. *Do other people put this much thought into the slang they use?*

The yard foreman waved at her as she hurried into the building, and Mr. Gaines nearly ran across the factory floor to meet with her. "Are you all right? I called Mr. Meyer's lawyer and asked what to do. He said to give him a ring if you weren't back soon. I was just about to make that call!"

With his slow, Southern drawl, it took the man the same amount of time to ask if she were all right as most people would have taken to make the entire "speech."

"They just dropped me off again." She began moving toward the painters' corner as she explained about the questions. "They'll probably bring photographs for us to look at." She hesitated and decided that most girls would definitely mention the murder. Clarice leaned a bit closer and did her best attempt at a whisper over the noise. "They say Mr. Meyer was *murdered*, and they think he died *here*. I might have been in the building with a killer!"

A few heads turned their way, and Clarice almost regretted it. Then again, if it drew sympathy that would prompt people to insist that she could never do something like kill kind Mr. Meyer, then well…

"I heard them say something that made me wonder if that's what they thought. They're keeping themselves mum, aren't they?"

Mum… is that slang?

"Miss Stahl?"

His question distracted her, and she stumbled over a rope on the floor. Mr. Gaines grabbed her just in time to prevent her falling but not before she'd turned red. "I'm sorry."

"They seemed to want all of our information, but they aren't saying much. Still, I think they suspect Miii—Emiliano Natale."

"That doesn't make sense. Without Mr. Meyer, Topo wouldn't get his nutcrackers."

Does he know…? Clarice decided to ask. "Why does a man like Mr. Topo want fifteen *thousand* nutcrackers?"

He shot her a look. Was it surprise? Amazement? Disdain? She could believe any of it. Then that familiar, gentle smile replaced whatever it was, and he urged her forward. "If you haven't worked that out, Miss Stahl, I'll leave you in ignorance. It may help with the police if you don't know."

At the painters' corner, instead of the never-ending stack of nutcrackers, her usual paintbox and brushes sat at her place. "Mary finished the necessary nutcrackers for you. We thought you might like a day of painting something more rewarding. You can resume work on the others on Monday."

The other girls beamed up at her, and it occurred to Clarice that they did like her. She'd always assumed that "tolerate" fit better, but the concern shown said otherwise. The moment she untied her coat, she had to rush off to hang it in the cloakroom, but upon her return, she reached for her smock and realized she'd been wearing it all along.

"Oh, now that is attractive…"

A ripple of giggles wafted around the table, and Edith spoke first. "So, how was it? Did you get Edisoned by the bulls about that bimbo?"

Edisoned… asked a lot of questions. She knew that one, of course. Bulls… well, she'd been right about that one, too. But bimbo? She hadn't heard that one yet.

Before she could ask, Mary snickered. "Did they figure out that you're his moll?"

Moll? Clarice blinked. "I'm sorry, who are you talking about? And what's a moll?"

By the looks on several of the other girls' faces, she wasn't the only one confused. That was a relief, anyway. Mary huffed. "Natale, of course. Everyone knows he's stuck on you."

"Well… that's a matter of opinion, but what's a moll?"

"Yeah," Edith pressed. "I've never heard of that. Doesn't sound very nice to call Clarice that. She's never done anything to you."

Mary threw back her head and laughed. "Moll… a tough guy's girlfriend. I mean, if you're not now, you will be. When a man like Milo Natale decides he wants a girl, he gets the girl."

Well, we'll see about that! Aloud, Clarice merely sniffed and said, "I think they're suspicious of him. They'll be bringing photographs of Mr. Topo's men for us to identify."

Mary blinked. "Why?"

"They were the last people to come before Mr. Meyer was killed, so the police want to talk to them."

"Oh."

She picked up a composite baby head with chubby cheeks and rosebud lips. Babies needed a gentle hand with the eyebrows. Too few, and they looked creepy. Too heavy, and the effect was clownish. "I like this new model. It's almost lifelike."

Across the table, Mary huffed at that one. "You wouldn't say that if you had to paint all those creases. At least they don't break as easily."

The girl worked with two brushes in one hand. One she used to apply a watery line of blush-colored paint in each crevice. The other she used to pounce most of that color out again.

She's improved while I've been distracted by all those ugly nutcrackers. After watching for a moment, Clarice picked up her brush with just a few fine, long hairs and swirled it in the paint before rolling off most of what she'd picked up. She smiled up at Mary and said, "You've gotten really good. I bet Mr. Meyer was proud of you."

The girl turned a greenish gray and swiped at her eyes.

"Thanks." A minute later, she set down her brush and the doll's head and bolted from the room.

Clarice paused mid swipe, ensuring she'd have to wipe off everything and start again, and asked, "Did I say something?"

"She's been on edge all morning." Edith shrugged. "Then again, I guess we all have. I'm just glad they didn't arrest you."

Is this where I say, "And how!"?

The usual conversation picked up again after Ann rose to go check on Mary. Edith's new fellow getting fresh after a date. "—told him, I said, Jerry, the bank's closed!"

That was a new one. After a few comments by the other girls, Clarice decided that it meant no "spooning," as one of the other girls called it. Clarice knew that one. The conversation then drifted to some drugstore cowboy who wouldn't leave Dotty alone.

"As if I'd be interested in a fellow who just hangs around looking for any doll he can sweet-talk. No thank you!" She giggled. "The cops are gettin' tired of him, too."

That sent the discussion into the rights and wrongs of how men tried to meet ladies in the first place, but Clarice wasn't interested. Instead, she revisited the events of the last twenty-four hours. *It wasn't long after now that Milo and the "bimbos"— what a silly word—came into the factory just one day ago.* Milo's wink, the creepy shadows and sounds, that noise... the person rushing past, nearly knocking her over...

She hadn't slept well, although she'd nearly fallen asleep in her plate. Arriving early and so cold, the police, Milo's concern for her. That had been sweet. He'd even watched out for her when the police took her.

We don't know who did this. We just know who didn't. I didn't, certainly. And Milo didn't. He couldn't have moved that body to his hotel room if we were running through the streets from Mr. Solari's gunmen.

Something about that didn't sit well, though. It felt as though she made an assumption she couldn't prove. But why? He hadn't been there to move the body. Why would he put a body in his room—even if he could have. Someone tried to make him look guilty. Didn't they?

No, he had to be innocent. He would have killed her if he'd killed Mr. Meyer. She could put him right there over the body. He had to know the police would talk to her. He wouldn't have let her live. He wouldn't have walked her home to keep her safe. He wouldn't have risked angering Mr. Topo.

Would he?

The squeaky wheels of the trolley announced the arrival of something, but Clarice was too lost in thought to bother. She had four heads left. It wouldn't be for her.

The chatter fell silent, however. Someone cleared a throat. When she looked up, her paintbrush poised over the hole where someone would cement in the doll's eye. Everyone wore excited expressions. "Surprise!"

Clarice turned, and on the trolley was a cake with a ring of mostly lit tall, stick-like candles around it. *Presumably twenty-seven?*

Someone set a note by humming, and the group all burst into, "For she's a jolly good fellow." Within seconds, half the factory had joined in if the clamor meant what she thought it did, but Clarice also suspected they didn't know whose birthday they celebrated. Mary called out, "Make a wish!"

She closed her eyes for a second, made that wish, and instead of blowing out each one, Clarice chose a long breathy sweep around the perimeter of the cake and a final puff on one stubborn flame. *Lord, may that wish be a prayer and Your answer be ours as well.*

———

CLUSTERED with the rest of the painters, Clarice exited the factory as the day ended, wishing she didn't have to return the next day. The first half of the year, employees worked five-day weeks. The second half they worked five and a half day weeks until Christmas. Just a few more weeks and Saturdays would be her own again. Only half the factories in Rockland were on the five or five and a half-day work week. *I'm fortunate—no, Brother Ellison says I should say* blessed. *I'm blessed to have half a day free on Saturdays.*

A strange feeling came over her, and Clarice surveyed the area, wondering what it meant. *I feel... watched.* She tossed that thought aside. *It's probably Milo. He'll show himself when I'm alone again.*

"I'm going to go get the special at the diner on 32nd Street. Who's coming with me?" Edith walked backward as she tried to convince everyone to join her. "Where's Mary?"

Dotty shrugged. "I was going to walk her way and see if she is all right. She sweet-talked Mr. Gaines into letting her go home—feminine reasons, of course. I know she lives alone with her father, and he's not likely to be sympathetic. I thought I could help her get supper for him. My brother doesn't get in until after eight anyway." Without another word, she took off down a side street.

Several other girls agreed to the diner idea, and even Clarice considered it. Mrs. Thacker, being a Catholic, always served fish on Fridays, and after missing lunch while at the police station, she knew fish wouldn't be enough. She could stop for crackers and cheese for later, or she could join the others for once.

"You'll be tempted to spend 'just a few cents' on small luxuries, Clarice. You mustn't let yourself do it. Each time it becomes easier to justify it 'just this time' until you're 'just broke.'"

Matron had sent her off with quite a few nuggets of wisdom, not all of which she had agreed with. Wearing garlic around her neck during flu season might keep away illness, but she suspected it was because it would keep away *people*. She'd have to wash well and trust Providence.

Well, this was one of those temptations. The group had gotten quite a bit ahead of her, and she'd almost called out to say she'd join them when a car pulled up beside her. A police car. Her heart sank.

The window rolled down, and a smiling Detective Doyle greeted her. "Heading home, Miss Stahl?"

"I am." Honesty forced her to add, "After I stop for a late-night snack. It's fish night, and I don't find it filling after a—" Heat filled her face. She glanced over her shoulder to see if the girls had gone on. They had. "Um, well it's just not very filling."

"And I suspect you had no noon meal. That was our fault." He put the car in gear and stepped out. "Would you let me take you for dinner? Something more lasting than fish? Maybe the diner over on—"

She'd nearly agreed, but at the mention of the diner, Clarice's mind cleared. "No!" Some part of her conscience began scolding. *You can't do that! What if he gets you to admit something! This is a ploy to learn more.*

"I see." The man had soulful eyes that looked sorry. "Well—"

"Please forgive me, Detective. I…" She gave him a weak smile. "The girls are planning to eat at the diner, and if I came in there with you… Well, you cannot imagine the teasing. They'd misunderstand, and…" Clarice stepped back. "But it was a kind thought. I appreciate it."

That smile turned lively and charming. He took her elbow and urged her toward the back of the vehicle. "Then how about Italian? Lombardi has made me a regular over at Vincenzo's. They make a spaghetti that will have you stuffed until morning—especially with their homemade bread. It's the yeastiest, crustiest bread you've ever imagined. Butter… garlic…" At the passenger door, he hesitated, one hand on the handle. "What do you say?"

Perhaps it was a ploy to learn more from her. That seemed likely, but maybe… just maybe she could do the same—gather information Milo could use to help clear their names. With that thought in mind, she smiled back at him. "I'd like that, Detective. Thank you."

As he opened the door and held it for her, the man flashed that smile at her again. "My pleasure, Miss Stahl. All mine..."

Oh, my!

NINE

The streets of Rockland grew noisier every day. Cars honking, trolleys clanging, bulls in their ridiculous uniforms blowing their infernal whistles anytime someone looked like they might be having a bit of fun... Between the bicycle bells and the newsboys shouting the day's headlines, Milo couldn't hear himself think, much less what those boys were saying.

Passing one and reading that headline for himself, however, nearly made him lose his lunch—or would have, if he'd eaten any. FACTORY OWNER KILLED BY NUTCRACKER.

He ran four blocks before he realized it could be talking about the broken doll in the office. There was no reason for anyone outside Solari's or Topo's goons to suspect him. No one had seen him in the factory except Clarice, and she hadn't told the police about him.

Had she?

It wasn't the first time he'd doubted her that afternoon, and seeing her go off with that bull Doyle... Oh, yes. Milo knew all about Eoin Doyle and his partner, of course.

Yes... Clarice Stahl absolutely could have killed Dietrich Meyer and returned when she heard a noise. Did he believe she had? Not really. But self-preservation required he consider it. He couldn't ignore the fact that he might be dizzy about a killer kitten.

And the bulls found Meyer in your hotel room, you mug. There's every reason for everyone to suspect you of everything.

Another kid in a flat cap and knickerbockers with a couple of heavy pullover sweaters waved his papers and called out the police's quest to find the missing "Nutcracker." Milo pulled out a nickel and passed it to the kid. He pulled out change, but Milo waved him off. "Get something hot on the way home, kid."

From there, Milo did the only thing he could think of. He went to the Rockland train terminus and found the men's lavatory. In there, he could lock himself in a stall and read the paper in relative privacy.

Lily Barnes had outdone herself, even writing about Clarice without knowing she had.

––––––––

WHILE THE WORLD prepares for the wonder of Christmas in these last weeks before the holiday, one family will be grieving. The large, family-like factory making the toys that many children hope to find under their Christmas trees received a terrible blow today. Dietrich Meyer, the owner of Meyer's Toys, was found dead late last night in a hotel suite at The Chesterfield Hotel.

Hotel sources state that room service was requested by the occupant of that room, Emiliano Natale. Emiliano is believed to be the notorious "enforcer" of the Topo Syndicate, otherwise known as "The Nutcracker." When the requested tray arrived, the room was empty save the corpse of Mr. Meyer.

Residents and guests of the hotel will be relieved to learn

that, although the police refuse to discuss their investigation, those who have overheard snippets of conversations state that they do not believe Mr. Meyer was murdered in the hotel room. While this may seem inconsequential with regard to anyone but those connected with the case, The Rockland Chronicle spoke to one young lady who had arrived for her new position as a companion to a guest to find out about the murder. She left quite distraught.

Much speculation is being made about this case. If Mr. Meyer was not murdered in the hotel room, then where did that deed take place? Why would he have been moved, and how? He wasn't a small man. Surely someone would have seen people carrying such a man through the hotel.

Furthermore, who murdered Mr. Meyer? Is the location of the body significant to identifying the criminal responsible? Did Emiliano Natale kill the man, and if so, for what purpose, and why would he move that body to his own room? Was he working for someone, or was it of his own volition?

At present, the police are left with more questions than they can hope to answer without speaking to Mr. Natale, but that is proving difficult. No one has seen him. When questioned about the man's whereabouts, a spokesman for the Topo Syndicate claimed that Mr. Topo had "a good business relationship with Mr. Meyer and would never have wished harm to a man necessary to the efficient running of our organization." And as far as Emiliano Natale, they did not know where the man was but would like to speak to him as well.

This statement implies that Mr. Meyer worked in connection with the syndicate, although the spokesman insists it is only a business transaction for "one of Mr. Topo's many enterprises."

Chief Thomas, of the Rockland Police force, states that finding Mr. Natale is of utmost importance. "Even if he is not responsible for this crime, he may have information that will help our investigation." That was all the chief said about

Natale, but he also strongly stated that if it is found that any organization was behind this murder, he would go after them with the full force of the law behind him.

The Rockland Chronicle hopes for the best, of course, but the criminal element in the city grows stronger every year and it cannot hold much confidence in the wake of so little effectiveness in the past.

THE ARTICLE SAID MUCH... and little. Clarice had been mentioned, of course. No one would know it was her. Relief hit a little too close to home on that score. *She's made you soft.*

The words that struck icy fear into Milo's heart and twisted it with the effectiveness of a knife were those chilling words, "would like to speak to him as well."

Speak... with a Tommy gun in a dark alley, most likely.

Only one option remained for him. He needed to leave town and be *seen* leaving so they'd leave the factory alone. Time for the 7:20 to Bloomington. From there he could go to Louisville, Chicago, St. Louis, or even all the way to Los Angeles.

A glance at his watch. 7:10. With the paper stuffed under his arm, he made his way out of the lavatory and to the terminus lobby. At one end, the ticket counters held rows of people lining up for last-minute fares. He needed to be the last one on the train—no time for the cashier to call for police.

Minute by minute, he moved from line to line, ensuring the longest wait. A few people gave him strange looks that sent Milo's heart racing until he realized his odd behavior probably prompted them more than anything.

At 7:16 he reached the window, wondering if he shouldn't

have let one more passenger go ahead. The platform could be crowded, though. That could delay him.

"I need a one-way to Bloomington." He fumbled for his wallet, laying the newspaper on the counter. *This better work.* Right then Milo decided that people who took up undercover work for government agencies were either brilliant or insane. "Sorry..." He fumbled for his cash and slid it across the counter. A glance at the newspaper told him he'd put it down right. Headline half showing—his police photograph faceup.

The cashier passed him the ticket and two dollars change. "Platform three."

"Thanks." Milo considered leaving the paper "accidentally" but feared the next customer might take it, and all the stress would have been for nothing. Instead, he passed it across. "Here you go. Won't need this anymore." He tipped his hat, grinned at the man, and took off through the crowd.

Clusters of people on the frigid platform made it difficult to get to where he needed to be, but that was just as well. The call for "all aboard" came just as he reached the end of the train, and he hopped on, moving inside to watch through one of the windows. A clang. A clank. The train jerked. The wheels groaned.

Movement. They'd just cleared the platform and were almost out of sight when he saw officers, two of them, burst through the crowd. Milo smiled and began making his plans as he turned around again.

IN THE RESTAURANT'S small dining room, a man with an accordion and another with a violin played music Clarice had never heard before. Heaping plates of noodles and a tomato and herb sauce had been placed before them within minutes of their entering the restaurant. The most enormous, delicious meatballs she'd ever dreamed of sat beside the mound of spaghetti, nearly mocking her idea of being "hungry." The hot bread must have just come from the oven, and the butter slathered over the top of its crusty shell held the hint of garlic in it.

Detective Doyle grinned and took the knife provided to saw through it. "Wait'll you taste this!"

"Who needs to taste? You could exist on the aroma alone!"

That grin only grew wider, if possible. "But who wants that when she can *eat* this!" He passed her a squashed slice of the steaming bread. "Delicious!"

In the doorway to the kitchen, a woman soothed a baby with a lullaby in Italian. Clarice's heart clenched. There'd be a baby for her someday... wouldn't there? A husband, a baby, a sweet little house with a small garden of flowers and vegetables? Snap peas, perhaps?

An idea formed and disappeared as quick as a flash of lightning, but in the illuminated moment, she'd seen someone there with her in that dream. Someone who looked a little too familiar for comfort. *Don't go getting any ridiculous ideas.*

Three bites into the most delicious food she'd ever eaten, the detective asked a question. "Did any of the other ladies remember anything after we left?"

Is this your idea of a subtle interrogation? Pretend kindness to put me off my guard? I'd begun to think better of you, Mr. Doyle. Almost immediately, she recanted her internal accusation. *It's his profession. He probably does it in his dreams. And you expected it.* Maybe she had, but the delicious meal had distracted her.

"Emily said she thought the officer with the scar on his chin looked like Mr. Natale but with paler skin." There. Now she'd see what he did with that.

"Nick? Interesting... but I see it." He speared another piece of meatball and considered it as if trying to decide which side to bite from. "The papers have all sorts of crazy theories going about everything." He gazed at her for a moment before taking that bite. When he finished chewing,

Detective Doyle added, "Only the Chronicle stuck to any semblance of fact."

"Oh, who wrote the article? Lily Barnes? She was so nice—"

"Who?" Doyle watched her, but Clarice took a bite and chewed it into oblivion as he watched. When he didn't keep speaking, she took another bite.

That worked. Doyle wiped his mouth and took a drink before acting as if he'd waited long enough. "That woman reporter? I think she did the article on Natale. What was she nice about?"

"Articles," Clarice blurted out. It might not have been what she had planned to say, but it was something she'd said often. "When she writes articles about bad people, she always puts some little piece in it that isn't bad—reminds us of their other side, my landlady says. I think it's good to remember that behind the criminal is a human being who has a mother or father who cherished them once."

"That's a kind but debatable thought. Many professionals in law will argue that not having parents who loved and nurtured their children is what drives some to a life of crime."

Clarice couldn't help but take up the mantle of devil's advocate. "Would that not mean that it is even more important to remind all of the best in someone before we turn them into irredeemable monsters in our minds?"

Whether because he chose not to argue over supper, or because he conceded some agreement, Clarice didn't know, but the rest of the meal continued in silence. Only as he escorted her down the steps of the little "*ristorante*" did the detective speak again. "That Mary seems to think you and Milo Natale have quite the thing going on. She called you his moll."

"I most certainly am *not!*" Clarice stopped in the middle of the sidewalk and stared at him. "Did you bring me here to try to weasel some non-existent information from me? I cannot be a fellow's girlfriend if I have not been introduced to him. Walking into a factory and winking doesn't constitute an introduction, much less a relationship, in my opinion." She began walking toward the trolley line. "I think I'll find my own way home, Detective. Thank you for the meal."

He reached for her arm and stopped himself from grabbing it just before she'd have stomped his foot for doing it. "Miss Stahl, I'm sorry. I don't know how to set aside my training. If a question comes up, I'll ask *the cat* if I think speaking it aloud will give me some insight."

Though she stepped back, Clarice didn't leave. She examined the detective's face before nodding. "I'd wondered about that."

"Let me drive you home." He led her to the car and opened the door. Before he closed it, the detective gazed down at her and said, "I really didn't think you'd be interested in a murdering bimbo like Natale. I just have to consider all statements. Can you see that?"

Though she nodded, Clarice clenched her jaw and her hands. *You're condemning a man without evidence. And I need to see him about it all.* She wanted to say "tonight," but opted for the next afternoon. *I need sleep. Good sleep.*

TEN

The early morning drizzle had slowed to a sputter and a spit by the time those who wished to attend Mr. Meyer's funeral were released to go. The rest of the employees were given an hour as well, so a fair number chose to spend their mini holiday away from St. Paul's Lutheran and the somber service within.

Clarice and several of the other painters sat on one of the rows in the middle of the large, cathedral-like church near the edge of the Hillcrest neighborhood. Leaded and stained-glass windows should have allowed in beautiful shafts of light, but instead, the panes seemed to weep the tears she felt she should have for a kind man who had treated her well from that first day. At the front of the room, behind the altar with its Bible and candles sitting atop a black mourning cloth, long pipes reached from floor to ceiling in places. Clarice had never seen anything so reverently beautiful.

As the mournful notes of the organ filled the room, she contrasted it with the simple church she'd attended for most of her life. The plain glass windows, the hard, scuffed pews, the lack of candles and other ornamentation. Even the music was so different. They sang to a piano sometimes, and other

times they just sang. There was a word for it that Brother
Ellison used, but Clarice had never asked him what it was—
something about occu-bella. She suspected Italian for "good,
plain singing."

I really need to remember to ask or even go look it up at the library.
Guilt shamed her at that thought. She'd come to mourn a
good man's life cut short, not to satisfy musical curiosity.

Edith leaned over and whispered, "Can't you just hear
Robbie Rogarth playin' jazz on that? It could be a scream!"
Her whispered, "scream" nearly was one, and someone poked
the girl from behind.

Clarice had to stifle a giggle when Edith turned around
and stuck her tongue out at the culprit with the alacrity of an
impish child. *Wouldn't Mr. Meyer have laughed at that!*

The pastor stood before them, praying a long, mournful
prayer about the wretchedness of man and his undeserving
state before a holy God. Just as Clarice thought there could be
no hope for mankind, no matter what she'd been taught to the
contrary, the man ended with, "We thank You for Your
merciful benevolence when we deserve Your powerful wrath.
Amen."

There is that, anyway.

While there might be something to be said for being
reminded of mankind's depravity, Clarice couldn't help but be
grateful that Brother Ellison leaned heavier on the wonder
that is the Lord's goodness and mercy to those who have
repented.

Out front, the hearse—horse-drawn and very fine, indeed
—waited for the mourners to follow it through the streets to
the Hillcrest cemetery. Clarice and Edith stood under the
oversized umbrella she'd found at a rummage sale a few weeks
earlier, waiting. "Let's skive off and get something to eat
before we have to return," Edith murmured under her breath.
"We don't need to get all soaked going to the graveyard. It's
creepy in there."

"It's daylight." To Clarice that solved the creepy factor, but Edith didn't seem to agree.

"There are still a bunch of skeletons just a few feet under our... well, feet! Gives me the heebie jeebies!"

Is heebie jeebies slang-worthy enough for me?

When Clarice didn't readily agree, Edith stepped out. "I hear the trolley coming. I'm going to scram and catch it. Coming with me?"

Clarice shook her head. "I'm staying." She nearly offered her umbrella, but her tendency toward colds reminded her of why she'd bought the large thing in the first place. "Will you be dry enough?"

"Sure. It's just spitting anyway. I'll dash between drops, just wait and see." With that, she was off, skipping puddles like a child after school and prompting scowls and smiles alike.

Clarice stood under the umbrella, out of the way, and watched the crowd for some sign of Milo. She hadn't seen him since Friday. *Tonight, ends one full week since Mr. Meyer died.*

What a week it had been, too. Running through the streets of Rockland with a mafia man, hiding that man out in her minister's home, being interrogated by police—*four times* now, no less—and now the funeral. *And we still don't know who killed him.*

The police were certain it was Milo, though. Every paper said so. For a girl who had never been much interested in newspapers, she devoured every one that arrived at her boarding house each morning before work. Being from the factory also made her a bit of a celebrity among the others, who all thought she looked for further mention of her own name. Clarice let them think what they would.

If they knew I wanted to be sure they hadn't traced Milo to Bloomington and arrested him... That's what the papers said. A ticket agent at the train station had positively identified Emiliano Natale as a man who had purchased a ticket, left a newspaper with his picture on the front page at his counter, and climbed aboard the train. *"I left my booth and followed him once I realized who it was—notified a bull—I mean, a policeman,"* he'd admitted.

When the train arrived at Bloomington, the police were waiting. But Milo hadn't been found, and Detective Doyle had been livid. *"Dumb fools thought they'd put him at his ease if they let him leave—make it less likely he'd harm someone. Instead, we lost him."*

The idea seemed sound to Clarice, but what—? Her thought broke off as a rather battered old pork pie hat bobbed along behind a cluster of women. *Is Mr. Ellison back so soon? That rumpled brim looks like his... then again, lots of men must sit on their hats or leave them lying on couches where others will sit on them.* Still, it looked like it might be the same one.

But Mr. Ellison was a tall man. This fellow wasn't. She took a step, curious now, but a tap on her sleeve changed that plan. Clarice turned to find a rather odd-looking but distinguished man nodding at her as if she'd said something he agreed with. "Miss Clarice Stahl?"

"Yes? That's me."

"Very good." The man had an accent that almost sounded English. Not quite, but nearly so. He passed her a card. "After the service, I am instructed to speak to you. I have information and a letter to discharge to your care."

Discharge to my care? That sounds either stuffy or ominous. I can't decide which. Aloud, she promised to arrive at... Clarice consulted the card. Hibbard, Hibbard, and Humphrey, 841 Hogarth Street, at one o'clock.

"Excuse me. I must find my supervisor and let him know I'll return late."

"Mr. Gaines has been apprised of the situation. I will see you at one o'clock, Miss Stahl. Thank you."

The mood shifted among the mourners. One moment they all stood about chatting in quiet but amiable tones and the next, they grew silent, somber, sad. The procession to the cemetery began.

As she stepped in line behind Mr. Gaines, Mr. Dalton, and

a gentleman she didn't recognize, Clarice marveled at the turnout and the ceremony. *What an old-fashioned thing to do—and perfectly fitting for him, too.*

THE OFFICE COULDN'T HAVE BEEN MORE different from the one Matron used at the home if it had been designed as a study in opposites. Instead of utilitarian white walls, these were paneled in rich dark wood and tasteful papers. The desk looked as though it had just arrived, unlike Matron's battered old thing with its carved and stained top. The files, the shelving, even the chairs—night and day.

But sitting there, despite being in the comfortable wingback chair instead of in the straight ladder-back ones in Matron's office, felt exactly as though Clarice had been called in for a scolding. The man seated behind the desk had eyebrows bushy enough to meet in the middle. For one crazy moment, Clarice expected them to shake... hairs? do an about face, and march ten paces back before... what? How did eyebrows battle? That they did, she had no doubt, but she couldn't be certain how it happened.

"I am sure you wish to know why I've called you here."

A line from a book she'd read once came to mind. Clarice couldn't recall the book, but the line had gone something like, "You want to tell me, and I have no objection to hearing it." Had it been a woman talking to her daughter?

Oh, bother. It will drive me to distraction until I remember now.

A glance up showed Mr.... Was he a Hibbard or a Humphrey? And had they deliberately chosen their office on Hogarth Street for alliterative purposes? *Now you're just being ridiculous.*

"Miss Stahl?"

Oh, he expects an answer. Why don't people just ask a question if they want a response? It's... well, it's enough to make a girl nerts!

Feeling rather pleased with how well she'd interjected slang into her thoughts, Clarice smiled up at the lawyer and nodded. "Of course." *Two can play this silly game.*

The man blinked as he put on spectacles, presumably the better to intimidate her with. She would not be so unsettled. She'd run from mobsters and seen dead bodies—well, one anyway. She could certainly withstand this man's worst.

"Yes." Mr. Humphrey—it had to be Humphrey. Only a man who looked like a perpetual harrumph, no matter how distinguished he might appear at first glance, should be named Humphrey. Regardless, the man drew out that word, "Yes," as if it had three syllables and a musical rest at the end.

Clarice almost took pity and asked what she could do for him, but the skeptical look he gave her put a stop to that nonsense. "Yes?" A niggling feeling in the pit of her stomach suggested she shouldn't enjoy creating a man's discomfiture nearly as much as she did. Still, she sat there, a perfect picture of serenity, if willing and attempting could make it so.

"I have here the will of Mr. Dietrich Meyer." He waved the document before him. "And here..." Mr. Humphrey (she hoped) passed one of the two envelopes lying on his desk toward her. "Is your copy. It is not the actual will, you understand. That will have to be filed with the court."

That made no sense. "Why would you give me a copy of Mr. Meyer's will?"

The man's hands pushed the other envelope across the desk. They were nice hands, firm, strong, without spots or wrinkles—much like the song they sang at church. "'*Tis a glorious church without spot or wrinkle, Washed in the blood of the Lamb...*"

"This is a letter from Mr. Meyer explaining that. You will read that first, please."

Mr. Humphrey may have tried to make his demand sound like a request, but he had failed, and the longer this interview went, the more contrary Clarice felt. "Perhaps I should take it home and read it in privacy."

"I would not advise that, miss."

The clock chimed the half hour. How had she been there so long already? The game would have to cease. She couldn't afford losing her position at the factory because she enjoyed discomfiting—was that a word?— a man like Mr. Humphrey. *You're becoming saucy, Clarice Stahl. Quite saucy.*

Clarice pulled the thick, creamy envelope toward her and broke a wax seal on the back. Dread filled her. A letter from Mr. Meyer? From the grave? If her hands shook a bit as she pulled pages from the envelope, could anyone blame her?

"Mr. Humph—"

"Hibbard—junior. Mr. Humphrey was my father's first partner."

This does not bode well for my powers of observation and deduction. Clarice cleared her throat and tried again. "Should I be concerned about the contents of this letter?"

"I think you will find it… surprising. Perhaps even a little disconcerting. But—"

Before he could make it any worse, Clarice unfolded the pages and began reading.

My dearest Clarice,

That was an odd beginning for a letter to an employee. Clarice shot a look at the misnamed Mr. Hibbard and immediately returned her gaze to the paper. The man looked like a cat who had just found a mouse in his cream.

If you only knew how many years of searching it took to find you.

. . .

CLARICE SHOOK HER HEAD, reread, and then searched for the date, which she'd ignored at first. Several years earlier. Wait, was that the date she'd begun working at the factory? Even stranger.

THERE ARE many things I need to explain, but in order to allay the dread of suspense, I will tell you the bare facts before I recount the story of why I looked for you at all. Clarice, my dear, your mother was my sister—the sweetest girl I ever knew until I found you and learned what sort of person you'd become.

You must have many questions about why I have not told you all this before, but suffice it to say, I had reasons to be cautious.

Hibbard will be giving you this letter, and with it, my will. You may expect that I will have left my estate to my nephew, Martin. It is what the world expects. It is never good for the world to become too confident in itself, is it?

Martin has a fine inheritance from his own father, his maternal grandfather, and another uncle on his mother's side. He does not need my money, my dear. You, however, were stripped of a normal life by me, your selfish father, and forgive me, your foolish mother.

Therefore, what Hibbard will tell you is that the house, the factory, my accounts, and my investments are yours, apart from a few specific legacies I've stipulated in the will. I ask that you keep the staff on at the house and retain at least Mr. Gaines at the factory until you know how to manage each place.

Now, let me explain why you knew none of this…

THERE, Clarice looked up and stared at Mr. Hibbard. "Is this some sort of cruel joke?"

"It is not." The man's eyebrows danced now, perhaps like fighters in a boxing ring. "As you will find when you finish the letter, he said nothing about his relationship with you as a means of protecting you. In his death, he knew he no longer could, although he hoped to live at least through Christmas so that obstacle could be overcome."

"Should what you just said be intelligible to me?"

This time the man smiled, and despite eyebrows that a caterpillar would envy, that distinguished air became exceedingly handsome. *You should smile more often.*

"I doubt it, but it will be." He rose. "Please relax with your letter. I'll give you a moment of privacy and request that my assistant bring us some tea." That smile broadened until a dimple appeared.

Oh, heavens! A dimple even. You'll make me goofy next! Clarice couldn't repress a smile at that thought. *I used slang without even thinking about it first!*

"Years of living in England," the man added by way of apology, she supposed. "It makes one long for a good cup on a dreary, draining day."

What is with you and your alliteration? When she realized he waited for an answer, she added, "Thank you."

Clarice did not begin reading when the door shut behind her. She sat in that chair, her head resting against the back and her thoughts swimming. One irrelevant one refused to leave her. *I suppose I need not be concerned about losing my position now.*

ELEVEN

The reality of her situation should have hit Clarice the moment she stepped outside Hibbard, Hibbard, and Humphrey on Hogarth Street. There at the curb waited Mr. Meyer's Duesenberg, with his driver standing ready to open the door for her. Clarice hardly noticed. She stared at the open door for a moment and just stepped in.

She answered his question about "home or factory" but couldn't have told anyone what that answer was. Clutched in her hands, the envelopes, but she still hadn't read all of the letter and had read none of the will. Instead, the thought, "*He was my uncle,*" repeated itself in her mind until she wanted to scream out her frustration and hurt.

How many years had she spent in the home when family had known where she was? How many holidays, birthdays, and that dreaded anniversary of her mother's death—the one everyone said she should forget, as if she could—had she spent alone on her cot, three beds from the window, in the girls' dormitory? How many times had she cried herself to sleep with only the, "shhh!" of the girls around her for comfort?

How many?

Halfway to the factory, rain began to fall once more. Clarice watched with morbid fascination as the distorted large brick building and truck yard came into view. She'd step out in a moment, and it would become clear again—drab, sad, but clear.

The truck yard boasted mud and puddles, but while men did their work in the rain, sploshing in and dodging the puddles, she was delivered right to the loading dock awning. So close, in fact, that Clarice didn't even need her oversized umbrella.

The driver, Holmes he said his name was, assured her he'd open her door and hurried out while Clarice marveled at the superfluity of names beginning with H that day. Holmes produced an unnecessary umbrella and held it over her as he opened the door.

"What time should I return to collect you?"

Clarice began to say, "Six o'clock, of course" when she realized that there was no "of course" about it. He could stay while she read the letter and then drive her to the house she would now call home. Mr. Hibbard had assured her she was expected. On the other hand, she could save that letter for when she arrived there, waiting to read it in some room that felt like an extension of Mr. Mey—that is, *Uncle* Dietrich.

She could need to be at the factory for mere minutes or even hours. The man's gaze met hers and she gave a weak smile. "I don't know."

"I'll wait over there, miss." He gestured to the corner where a lone tree grew. "I'm out of the way over there."

A vague sense of familiarity formed at that thought. Yes... hadn't she seen that car sitting there when she arrived and still sitting there when she left sometimes? "Holmes, what do you do when you sit there all day?"

"I go to Paris, miss. Or sometimes Egypt. I climb Mount Everest or dive deep into the ocean and discover hidden worlds."

A vague sense of, *I should know what he means,* filled her, but she didn't. Instead, she stared at him before nodding. "How nice for you."

A low chuckle caught her as she'd turned to go. Looking up at him, she caught a twinkle in the man's eye. "I read, miss. Never used to do it. Always thought reading sounded rather dull, but one day Mr. Meyer said, 'Holmes, there's nothing duller than staring out of an automobile window at a brick wall. Try it.' And he gave me a copy of *Around the World in Eighty Days.* After that, I didn't dread those long days anymore."

As she walked away, Clarice mocked herself. *Read. Of course, he reads. Goes to Paris or Egypt. Dives into the ocean.* That thought pulled her up short. She turned and called out to Holmes as he opened his door again. "The book where you found hidden worlds in the ocean? What was that?"

"*A Thousand Leagues Under the Sea.* You'll find it in Mr. Meyer's library— three shelves to the left of the door, middle shelf, third from the left side. I'll put it on his desk for you if you like."

"Thank you." Only once she'd entered the factory did Clarice realize her response was not a reply. Hopefully the man could translate her befuddlement into the request she'd meant it to be.

The whirl of the large drilling machine, the clank of the scrapers, and the squeak of conveyor belts assaulted her as she entered the belly of the factory. How had the noise ever become so familiar as not to notice? *I noticed the silence that night. It bothered me.*

Mr. Gaines greeted her as he came out of the painters' corner, pushing a trolley of completed nutcracker dolls. Clarice examined them and winced. "Who is doing these?"

"Mary. Rather fine for a new task, I'd say."

Clarice wouldn't. The outer rim she'd done instinctively from day one was missing, and the dolls looked incomplete without it. "I mixed a little blue and black paint together and created an outside rim to the iris. Would you have her do that, please? They should be consistent, don't you think?"

"Mr. Topo doesn't care if they have it or not," the man protested.

An examination of the back of the doll showed the MT logo on the underside of the lever. "It'll have our logo on it, though. Someone seeing something missing will attribute it to us, not the person who ordered the lot. Don't you think we should be consistent?"

"If that's what you want, Miss Stahl." He wheeled the trolley back into the painters' corner and Clarice followed, unbuttoning her coat as she went.

When she reached for her chair, Mr. Gaines cleared his throat. "Um, Miss Stahl?"

"Yes?"

"I think Mr. Dalton is expecting you up in your office."

"My off—" Understanding tossed her into a swirling vortex of vertigo. Clarice gripped the back of the chair and held on. "Oh... I see."

"Her office?" Edith sat up and pointed her bushy brush at Clarice. "Did you get a promotion?" She turned to the others. "Maybe she did bump off the old coot! Smart thinkin'!"

"Um..." For reasons she couldn't fathom, Clarice was loath to explain.

Mr. Gaines had no such trouble. "Miss Stahl is now the owner of Meyer's Toys. Show a little respect, Miss Fischer."

Someone whistled low. Edith just gaped. A glance around the room showed some whispering, others glowering, and only Mary and sweet Emily looking genuinely pleased for her. Then one of the whispers reached her.

"...always knew she was up to no good being called up to his office all the time. Now we know."

Before Mr. Gaines heard the speculation and overreacted, Clarice thanked them for their work and promised to be back helping the next day. Edith snorted. "Well, you'll be here alone unless you're makin' us work on Thanksgiving now."

To hide her shaking hands, Clarice shoved them in her coat pocket and addressed the group. "Oh, yes. I'm sorry. I am a bit disconcerted, as I'm sure you understand." She turned to Mr. Gaines and said, "Perhaps we can allow everyone to leave an hour early today—for the holiday. A show of respect as it were."

The man wanted to argue, but Clarice turned to make her way through the factory before he could say something to convince her to reconsider. And he could. Even as she strode past the boxers and the assemblers, she realized that paying for an hour of labor from which she received no work… *and* for seventy-five employees… *What have I done!*

She'd economize, of course. That's what she'd do. Just as soon as she found a way to do it. Perhaps Dalton and Mr. Gaines would have suggestions.

Mr. Gaines reached around her and opened the door to the office. An unspoken rebuke lingered between them, and Clarice decided to address it. "I was rash, Mr. Gaines. That was an expensive decision—one I had no right to make. However, I won't rescind it. You'll have to show me ways to economize to make up the difference." She offered him a weak smile. "I hope you'll forgive me. It won't happen again."

Dalton was on the telephone, assuring someone that the order wouldn't be late, despite the unfortunate demise of Mr. Meyer. After a few uh-huhs, and another mmm-hmmm, he said, "I'm sure the new owner will be pleased to meet with you on Friday."

Clarice waved her hands at him to stop him, but Mr. Dalton ignored her. "Thank you for your patience, sir. We'll see you then. Yes, thank you."

The man fumbled for a handkerchief to wipe his brow as he set the receiver in its cradle. A mumbled buzzing filled her ears, but Clarice couldn't understand what he said. All she could do was stare at a small metal bowl with candies in it—candies wrapped in that new, clear cellophane. Mr. Meyer had touted it as perfect for preserving freshness and keeping germs at bay.

"Just you wait," he'd said. *"Someday, they'll wrap everything from cookies to children in cellophane."*

"May I have a candy?"

The buzzing ceased. Clarice glanced at both men who now stared at her. Mr. Dalton nodded. "Of—of course." He lifted the bowl, offering it both to her and Mr. Gaines.

Clarice felt like an idiot until she'd unwrapped the piece. Even before it touched her tongue, she knew what it was. Peppermint.

TWO MEN STOOD on either side of the door to a tearoom just two blocks from The Chesterfield. He'd checked the back, and two men guarded that exit as well. Angelo stood smoking a cigarette and flirting with a girl on the other side of the window. Had it only been him, Milo might have chanced a quick word.

But Angelo had been paired with Carlo. *This is retribution for flirting with Therese. If you hadn't done that, he wouldn't still wanna kill you.* All the self-recrimination wouldn't help him now, though.

They'd come to the tearoom straight from Meyer's funeral service. Milo had enjoyed watching the discomfort of the Catholic men sitting in the Protestant church and not knowing the order of things. No incense, no confessionals, no kneeling and rising.

For his part, he'd liked the service until that final prayer. Milo had squirmed through every word of it. Through every long, agonizing second of it.

Risking everything to find where they'd go next? It might

have been crazy, but he needed to do something. Time was running out.

Then Gio had rushed up to Mr. Topo and whispered something to him. The boss had gone cold, hard, and nearly white. Even now Milo shuddered at the remembrance.

So, he'd followed them here, wondering what he could learn or even if he could learn anything. Angelo stomped out his cigarette and turned to say something to Carlo. The man shrugged. But a conversation began, and Milo needed to hear it.

A group of businessmen walked toward him, likely heading to the hotel for a lunch meeting. Milo needed to join them and fast, but if he ran, one of the boys would notice. Staying calm and unaffected—the hardest part of hiding out from people who wanted to kill you.

Just in front of him, a woman started to cross the street, and he stopped her in time to prevent her from stepping in a deep puddle. This would work. "Excuse me. There's a hole there. You'll go down into it. Over this way…"

She wore one of those close-fitting hats that made it impossible to see a woman's face unless she looked directly at you. And she did. Bright eyes smiled at him. Pink cheeks. Reddish brown hair. Stylish, too. "Thank you. Very kind of you, I'm sure." Her voice would melt iron.

"Let me escort you across the street. It's treacherous in this weather."

"I imagine." Her "I" sounded more like, "ah."

"You aren't from here."

Laughter that sounded like deep church bells rang out. Milo would have clapped a hand over her mouth if he thought it would help. Instead, he pulled down the pork pie hat he'd borrowed from the minister and led her around another puddle and just a few feet away from where Carlo stood, back to him.

"I'd say you aren't either," the woman said as they reached the sidewalk.

It took Milo a moment to catch her meaning. "Born just twelve blocks away, actually. Have a nice day."

He joined the group of men as they passed Carlo and Angelo and strained to hear anything he could. Most was drowned out by the chatter of the businessmen, but he heard one thing sent chills through him.

"—Dalton says that doll Milo's dizzy about inherited everything."

TWELVE

Holmes turned the car into a long, tree-covered driveway. Most of the leaves had fallen, but a few clung to their twigs as if refusing to release for anyone or anything. As the driveway curved, she tore her eyes from the mental vision of how beautiful the trees must be in the other months and gaped at the sight of the house.

I thought houses like this had names like Elmhurst or Brookfield. Perhaps I should call it "Fortuna."

"Welcome home, Miss Stahl. I'm sorry this is what brought you…" Holmes turned to look over the seat at her. "Sometimes Mr. Meyer talked to me—like a friend. He mentioned you, although he never told me your name. It hurt him that he couldn't bring you here."

Not enough, apparently. Though she told herself she was being unkind, Clarice decided that she *felt* unkind. A lonely childhood might have been avoided if her uncle had *been* an uncle to her.

Holmes didn't see her to the door. He hopped back in the car and drove around the house and out of sight before she knew what had happened. There she stood in the rain, gazing up at a house bigger than any she'd ever seen, much less entered. What the style was, she couldn't identify. Three floors —or was there a small fourth at the top? Imposing. Lots of windows with arches over each one—rounded, not peaked like at the Lutheran church. Bleached brick and stone.

It may have been beautiful, but something about it seemed cold and hard, too.

Double doors flanked by floor to ceiling windows covered in what looked like heavy drapes left her without any idea of the house inside. Did she knock? Just walk in?

Before Clarice could decide, the door opened and a woman wiping her hands on her apron spoke. "Oh, dear me, miss. You must be Mr. Meyer's niece. Mr. Hibbard called to say you'd be coming. I hadn't planned for a supper, what with everyone gone." She beckoned for Clarice to enter. "Come in, come in. You'll catch your death out in that cold and damp. Now everyone was given the afternoon off, what with the funeral and all. My man and I live here, though, so we were just going to have our supper and rest in our cottage until I got that call."

On and on the woman prattled until Clarice wanted to beg her to stop. She'd made beef pies and creamed peas for supper. Would that do for miss? Miss would want to see Mr. Meyer's library and study first, wouldn't she? They were famous… how, Clarice couldn't tell. But the woman whose name she still didn't know insisted they were, so that's all that mattered.

Outside a dark paneled door, the woman paused. "This was Mr. Meyer's study. He spent most of his time in here. If you go through the frosted doors, you'll find the library if you prefer that. Supper's in two hours, if you don't mind. And what color do you prefer? Yellow or blue?"

"Color?" Clarice couldn't see why it mattered.

"I'll just put you in the yellow room for tonight. They're the only two kept ready for guests, so I thought to ask. The yellow room will be cheerful for you after a day like today."

The woman pointed at the desk over by a window. "There's an electric buzzer there that connects the telephone to the kitchen. If you need something, just lift the receiver, and push that button. I'll hear you." She turned to go.

"Um, Mrs...." Clarice tried to steady her voice. "I'm sorry, I don't know your name."

"Oh, saints preserve us, I've gone and lost my head. I'm Mrs. Grueber. Mr. Meyer always called me 'Grubby,' and you can too, if you like."

What an extraordinary nickname! Clarice just smiled. "Thank you. I, um..." She pulled the envelopes from her pocket. "I have a few things to do, so if you need me, I'll be in here or in the other room. Where would I find a washroom if..."

"Down the hall at the very end. Can't miss it."

And with that, the woman was gone.

Several scents mingled in the room. Something slightly earthy, which Clarice thought might be the ferns. Perhaps someone had watered them recently. A faint sweetness served as an undertone to ink and woodsmoke. When she sat at the desk, she found the source. Pipe tobacco.

She picked up a pouch and sniffed. Fruity, a bit of floral, a touch of spice. Cigars and cigarettes stank. She had her fill of them out in the yard at the factory, much less anywhere else, but this... Clarice inhaled another whiff. "It smells like him."

And yet she'd never known Mr. Meyer smoked a pipe. She'd never seen him, anyway. *That's something a niece should know about her uncle.*

What if he'd been wrong? What if he'd left his life's work and savings to the wrong young woman, and there was someone out there who should benefit?

Lowering herself into the rich leather chair, Clarice pulled the letter from its envelope and decided she'd start where she left off. "Then I'll ask to see where he kept family portraits. A family like this should have one of Mama. And I can still see Mama's face if I concentrate hard enough."

Though she'd intended to continue reading as though she hadn't stopped, Clarice began again, taking note of each word until she found that place once more.

—————————-

WHEN I WAS JUST twenty-five and my brother and I had come to America to seek our fortunes, we left our sister with an aunt in our little village in northern Germany. It took a few years, but my small store where I made each toy myself grew busy enough that I needed a bigger workroom—employees. My brother Karl went into banking. In less than ten years, I had a small factory down by what we used to call the Dry Docks area, and he had risen to manager of his bank.

Our aunt died, and Luisa, then just eighteen, needed to come to us. I was a busy man and didn't keep a close enough eye on her. Karl was married and had social responsibilities, so Luisa was left much to her own devices. After just six months here, Hans Stahl had claimed her heart.

I refused the marriage. Dear Clarice, I would refuse again today, but I would do it with more gentleness and understanding. I would offer hope. Then, I was harsh and so very certain of my rightness, and Karl trusted that I knew what I was about.

You will guess the rest. She ran off with Hans. I don't know how they did it, but they evaded my attempts to find them. I learned eventually that in 1906, when Germany did not fare well at the Algeciras Conference, he left Luisa without any money to support the two of you and took a ship home to Germany, confident there would be war and determined to fight for the motherland. Eight years later, he was proven correct, but by then, your dear mother had died. I have never found him. He may have died in the war.

I spent those years looking for you all. Back then, I hadn't made the money I have now. I was comfortable but not wealthy. Only when a detective I hired discovered a death certificate in your mother's name did I give up hope of seeing her again.

The search went on for you.

Just as I found you, Mario Topo visited my factory. I thought he was there to require protection payments. No one would hurt our machinery or my employees in exchange for those payments or some such thing. I'd heard of it from other factory and store owners. I wish that this were all he required.

It was the day that the headlines read "United States Goes Dry" that the detective found you and Mr. Topo found me. He's a shrewd businessman, Clarice. Never underestimate him.

I thought his large and rather strange order would be that —a single order. So, I decided to wait to meet you. Once he was out of my life, then I would retrieve you from the home and install you in mine. I would introduce you to the world as my niece, and our family would have a piece of Luisa back again.

But Mario Topo liked our "arrangement" as he called it. When I tried to refuse to meet his demands, Martin was beaten on the way home from school. I couldn't risk him knowing about you, so until I could divorce myself from this unwanted "arrangement," I ensured you were safe at the home, that the children in the home had plenty to eat and enough coal to keep warm, and I prayed like I've never prayed before that there would be some way out of this.

Then the matron of the home contacted me, telling me that you were too old to keep there anymore. She'd heard comments from people that unsettled her. So, you came to work for me, and I was forced to try to pretend you meant no more to me than any other employee. This was not easy, my dear.

If you're reading this letter, it means I have died before extricating myself from Topo's clutches. Beware of him. Don't cross him. It would probably be best to sell the business and leave Rockland. Go somewhere sunny, warm, and safe. Regardless, be happy and know that you were beloved by a foolish man who thought he could protect you by keeping silent.

Forgive me, my dear. Forgive me but stay safe. You are in a very dangerous position. Never forget that.

With love,

Your uncle, Dietrich Meyer

———————

A DOOR BANGED SOMEWHERE, and a voice called out, "Grubby? Where is she? Where is that—?" A few unsavory words drifted into the study, but before Clarice could rise and make it to the door, a man's silhouette filled it. He stepped into the light.

Martin Meyer. "You little gold-digger. I won't let you get away with it. I'll kill you first."

He swayed, and he might have fallen, but Mrs. Grueber appeared behind him. "Turn around, Martin."

Martin nearly fell as he tried to turn, but the woman's hand striking his cheek seemed to snap him out of his rage. He wept, wailing about things Clarice couldn't understand, but she did understand one thing he said, and the words made no sense at all. He said, "She killed him."

———————

THE DINING ROOM OVERWHELMED HER. Perhaps it was the enormous table with its dozen chairs for one person. Maybe it was how small that table looked in such an enormous room. Mrs. Grueber bustled in with a tray and set it on the table beside Clarice with a bit of a thud. "Begging pardon, miss. I'm still a bit put out at young Martin. No need to take it out on you and the china, is there?"

"I don't know who he thinks I killed, but—"

"Oh, I doubt he meant anything by it. He found some liquor somewhere and it turned his head. Perhaps he meant it was the search for you, or perhaps he meant some other 'she.' We won't know until he wakes. I've put him in his usual room. I hope that's all right."

"Of course!" To herself Clarice added, *He's family. Isn't he?*

The beef pies were so much more than the simple name implied. Clarice's mouth watered in a most unbecoming fashion as Mrs. Grueber slid one onto a plate for her and followed it with bread, peas, and a creamy soup. "It isn't much. I forgot to bring the soup out in time, so it's a bit of a hodge-podge. I hope you understand. We'll have a proper Thanksgiving supper for you tomorrow."

"Will you be eating? How about the rest of staff? Do they have somewhere to eat a good meal?"

The woman stopped ladling soup and stared. "Why, of course. And my Henry and me, we'll be eating at the cottage after you and the family's had your meal."

Clarice's complaint about yet another "H" in her life fizzled at that last statement. "The family?"

"They always come for Thanksgiving because they have Mrs. Meyer's family for Christmas, you see."

"They're coming? Here? Tomorrow?"

Mrs. Grueber nodded. "Of course—" She stopped mid-sentence and stared. "Unless you'd rather I send a note saying you aren't up to it. Holmes can drive the meal over, and I can—"

Clarice picked up her spoon and dug into the bowl as she interrupted. "No, no. I just…"

A family dinner. She had one decent dress for such an occasion—not quite fine enough, but the home had been particular about that point. Every girl left with a new work dress, good, sturdy work shoes, and one quality black dress for "occasions" as Matron put it. Boys left with a good suit and an outfit of work clothes, compliments of a "generous benefactor."

"I'll have to sponge my dress, I suppose. What time should I be—oh, no. You were making up—that is, have a room made up for me. But I have nothing here. I need to go back to my room at the boarding house. My clothes and things..."

"Make a list and write a note for your landlady. Holmes will drive around and pack it up for you. It's his job," she added when Clarice would have protested.

Another question formed and dissolved with the first bite of a beef pie whose crust disintegrated at the touch of a fork. She would eat a good meal, go into her uncle's library—*her* library, that is—and think. *I have so many things to think about.*

"I'll let Holmes know to be ready for your list at... seven o'clock?"

Even as she nodded her agreement, Clarice's thoughts continued. *Think and plan, I suppose.*

The meat pie disappeared before she knew what had happened. Clarice pulled the soup bowl closer and found it empty as well. Peas had never been her favorite, but a grumbling stomach demanded more, so she ate them and the dinner bread as well. She'd been about to rise when Mrs. Grueber returned carrying a plate of chocolate cake the size of which Clarice had never seen!

"I reckon you haven't had a good meal today, what with the funeral and all. I thought you could use something sweet. It's my Henry's favorite. He used to like to claim his mother's sacher-torte was the best dessert ever made, but I gave him a piece of cake one afternoon, and he asked me to marry him on the spot."

"I can imagine why. This looks heavenly!" That first bite dissolved in her mouth without the need for chewing. "Oh, my…"

"There is more in the kitchen under the dome on the table if you get peckish in the night. Will there be anything else?"

She started to shake her head, her mouth being too busy absorbing the deliciousness of that cake, but a thought stopped her. Clarice held up a finger and swallowed. "Oh, yes. Where do I bring my dishes when I'm done? I don't know where that kitchen is."

The woman gave her a genuine smile as she scooped up the dirty china. "You just go out the door and turn left. Walk until you find yourself in the warmest room of the house. It's fine in the cold months and miserable in summer."

The cake disappeared almost as fast as Mrs. Grueber and her supper. It felt rude to leave dirty dishes at the table, but halfway down the hall to the kitchen, Clarice felt awkward arriving with them and scurried back to leave them at her place. *Maybe when I've been here a while.*

She stopped by her uncle's desk on the way to the library. With a few sheets of paper and an envelope in hand, she grabbed his fountain pen and at the last moment, the tobacco pouch. With care not to wrinkle the paper, she carried it all to the frosted pocket doors the separated study from library and jostled things until she could unlatch the doors and nudge them apart.

The light from the study sent warm glows and shadows through different corners of the room. A reading lamp stood in the middle of a library table, so Clarice dumped everything there and pulled the chain. Warm amber light filled the space, and the room took on an even lovelier quality. Rows upon rows of spines—beautiful ones with gold foil and filigree work tooled into leather—stared back at her as if daring her to skip all the responsible things she knew she should be doing and lose herself in the pages of a book.

As a young girl, she'd loved to make her way to the Carnegie Library, enter the beautiful building with its rows and rows of books, pick out the allotted two she could borrow, and race home to their little flat to lose herself in the world of Oz with Dorothy and Toto or that of the pirates in *Treasure Island.*

At the home, reading had become a luxury for the classroom alone, and since moving away from there, Clarice hadn't let herself take up that habit again. You never knew when the joy of it might be stripped away.

She flicked away a tear and pulled out the sheets of paper. The fountain pen was a fine one—hefty and solid. Beautiful. Every sound the house made sent her into jitters that Clarice finally attributed to her using something without permission. *But it's mine now, as strange as that is.* Hers or not, it didn't *feel* like it, and feelings always demanded an audience, even at the expense of truth.

Instead of an itemized list, something that she likely couldn't do, Clarice wrote a short note to Mrs. Thacker and explained the change in her circumstances. She requested that Holmes be allowed to retrieve her things and asked that the woman be certain he looked under the bed and in all the drawers. She closed the letter with gratitude for the woman's kindness and, at the end, added a postscript.

P. S. I would appreciate it if you would hold my room for me until after the first of the year. Holmes will give you the rent through then. Between us, I don't trust this windfall. You can reach me at the factory any time you like or at Mr. Meyer's home. Holmes will have the address. Thank you.

With that settled, she hopped up to find an envelope and seeing the buzzer, lifted the receiver and pressed it. Mrs. Grueber's voice came on the line almost immediately. "Yes, miss?"

"Is there some sort of household account I might borrow from until mor—that is, Friday? I need to give Holmes money for Mrs. Thacker."

"Certainly. But you don't need to borrow from yourself, dear. You look in the third drawer to the right. There's a leather pouch there with everything you could need, and if not, there's a safe."

The pouch was there, and so was enough money to keep her landlady satisfied. Thirty dollars would reserve the room through the first of the year. She could revisit it then.

Clarice punched the buzzer again and picked up the receiver. When had she put it down? No one came on the line. She pressed it again, slowly, carefully. Mrs. Grueber came on. "Find it, dearie?"

"Yes. Where do I go to give this to Mr. Holmes?"

"He'll be right in to get it. You stay put. It's frightful out there!"

While she waited, Clarice pulled another sheet of paper toward her and began scribbling notes about everything. The night Mr. Meyer had been killed. The next day at the factory, with the police, with Detective Doyle. Mr. Ellison at the funeral. Peppermints on Mr. Dalton's desk. Martin Meyer's illogical assertion that "she," whoever that was, had killed Uncle Meyer.

"Where is Milo?" she whispered to herself. "Maybe he could make sense of this."

She went over the list again, her mind insisting she'd found something but whatever that something was remained elusive. Every second of every day flashed before her. She captured memories, held them, and pondered them before allowing them to race on as if on the wings of the fastest bird in the world.

Five minutes after Holmes had retrieved the note and promised to return promptly, Clarice stared at a line she'd drawn on the paper. A simple line between a hat and a missing Milo.

THIRTEEN

E yes closed, mind racing, Milo lay on the bed, a million thoughts fighting for preeminence. She'd inherited. How? Why? What prompted a man like Dietrich Meyer to leave his house, his money, and his company to a factory worker?

Rumors raced through the underbelly of Rockland, and every one of them made his blood boil. *Who can know what those crazy Germans will do?*

Then again, he didn't know Clarice Stahl beyond observing her on a regular basis—that and a madcap race through the city to avoid being gunned down. Meyer could have been her sugar daddy. Enough dolls had them these days.

He just wouldn't have believed it of her.

Milo shook himself and tried to concentrate. Wondering about things he couldn't change wouldn't help him decide how to survive. Then again, if he knew she was guilty, he'd leave town and set up somewhere else. He had the dough. His eyes opened and he looked around the dark room, picking out the furniture in the night shadows.

A little over twenty-four hours. Then he had to get out of there and stay away this time. The Ellisons would be back.

Where he'd go… he didn't know. Maybe that was the answer. If he didn't find some proof of Clarice's innocence, he'd leave.

The front door rattled. Milo caught his breath and sat up. His heart raced, and his mind chased after it. Home so soon? How would he explain? Or would they come in that room? Maybe if he hid…

He crept from beneath the covers and smoothed them back over the bed. It wasn't how he'd found it, but maybe Mrs. Ellison hadn't seen how it looked before she left and would assume he was just no good at making a bed. His feet slid into his shoes, and as tempted as he was to leave them untied, he didn't.

Footsteps. Milo's heart should have exploded from overwork. Where were the voices? If they were coming home, wouldn't they…?

A shiver ran through him. Topo's men had found him. He'd be lying on the floor when the Ellisons returned unless Topo wanted him found sooner. That poor woman.

If he hid, maybe they would think he wasn't there. The rattle had come from the front, so perhaps a sprint down the hall and out the back door. Except his coat hung on the tree by the front door, and all of the bimbos would recognize it.

The doorknob twisted, so Milo dashed behind it. Perspiration coated him, but he was determined to die fighting for his last breath. A creak pierced the air with the effectiveness of a scream as the door swung open. Milo prepared to grab the goon's throat just as a soft voice whispered, "Milo?"

He hadn't had time to stop himself. His arm had the "intruder" in a chokehold before he heard his name—and who said it. Dropping his arms, he squeezed back against the wall. "Clarice?"

"I figured out where you were." A cough followed. "I suppose I could have rung you up, but I don't suppose you'd have answered."

"And the Ellisons don't have a telephone."

Clarice just blinked at him. "They didn't approve the installation? What a shame. I think it would be helpful."

He wanted to ask what she meant, but they didn't have time. If Topo's men were following her, as he felt certain they were, they'd be inside in no time. "We hafta go. You were probably followed."

"Hopefully, they followed Holmes back to my boarding house, then."

He didn't have time to ask what she meant. Milo just rushed out, grabbed his coat, and pulled his hat on. "You came in the front?"

"Yes—"

"Lock it. We'll go out the back."

She harumphed. "I'm glad I put the key back before coming in, then."

So am I. But he didn't say it. Instead, he pulled her through the house and out the back door, taking care to lock it as he did. The backyard was draped in shadows. All of them moved in the night wind, and that didn't bode well for catching sight of someone before they attacked.

"I really—"

Milo clapped his hand over her mouth and whispered low in her ear. "No." He had to hope she'd know what he meant.

They scrambled over hedges and dashed through back yards, rousing every dog in the neighborhood, of course. And all for nothing. By the time they reached the trolley, it was obvious. No one had followed them.

"We should walk," he argued as she pulled coins from her purse. "Trapped on a trolley..."

"We must beat Holmes home," she argued. Then she stared up at him. "How is a place I've spent just a couple of hours in something I now call home?"

He'd like to know that himself, but they didn't have time to philosophize. "Why do we hafta beat him?" Despite his reticence, he climbed up onto the trolley without further argument.

"He'll bring my things up to my room. And I won't be there. He'll go back to the library… and I won't be there. I need to be there, or it'll be suspicious, don't you think?"

A shrug seemed safe enough.

"I should have thought of it before I left. I could have waited until he got back."

Once on the trolley, Milo lost all ability to converse naturally. Maybe it was sitting in the corner as if sweethearts on the way home from an evening out. It was obvious that was what the woman down the aisle from them thought. She kept sending them sweet smiles as if imagining all the romantic little nothings he must be saying.

Milo had already decided he'd never manage that sort of thing again. He'd heard folks talk about being "tongue-tied" for much of his adult life. In his heart, he'd mocked those who were. Not anymore. The knots in his stomach had tied more in his tongue for good measure.

What it did do was solidify in his mind and heart one vital thing. Clarice Stahl had not seduced Dietrich Meyer. Nor had the reverse occurred. She hadn't killed the old guy. So, she'd be a target, and it was his duty to protect her.

Now to figure out how to do that.

They switched trolleys twice until they reached the swanky end of town. Folks on this side of Rockland had expansive yards with gates, walls, hedges, shrubs, and trees. They kept to the shadows of all these and only twice had to duck and hide. Clarice froze each time, but she relaxed as the car passed. "Not him," she added each time.

Mr. Topo's house was half the size of the house Clarice turned into. "How do we get—?" She froze at the sound of a car coming.

"The back. Let's go."

"But what—?" Clarice started to protest, but Milo

grabbed her hand and raced down the side yard toward the back. Near what he hoped was the kitchen door, he ducked behind a woodpile.

"Must like their hires fere. Go in. Fast. Get upstairs."

"But—"

He gave her a shove before dropping down again and hissing, "Go!"

Clarice shot one unreadable look back at him and skipped up the steps and out of sight.

Mother of God, be with her. He hadn't prayed in earnest for years, but it sounded like something his mother had prayed often. Mr. Ellison had insisted he pray, so hopefully God would listen since the prayer was for someone else. *Please.*

THE AROMA of pumpkin pie greeted her as Clarice slipped through the back door. The warmth of the kitchen reached all the way to bones she hadn't realized were achingly cold. From her place at the stove, Mrs. Grueber shot her a confused look. "I didn't see you go out."

"Oh, I went out the front door. I needed to think and walk a bit. It's starting to rain again, though, so I thought I should come inside." Her fingers trailed across the worktable as Clarice inched toward the door. "Sure smells delicious in here. Don't you ever have a chance to put your feet up?"

"In just a few minutes, I'll be heading back to our cottage, dearie. My man's probably wondering where his cocoa is, but if I get some of this finished now, it's less to do in the morning." She eyed Clarice before saying, "There are towels in the linen closet—the last door on the left before you reach the bathroom. It's just a few doors down from your room. Yours is the one with the open door."

"Oh, a bath! That sounds heavenly. When Holmes arrives,

I'll have to do that. What a lovely idea." She hesitated. "Mrs. Grueber?"

The woman looked up at her from where she sat stirring something in a bowl. "Everything all right?"

"Holmes? Should I give him a tip or something? I don't know how this works."

"His wages are paid every Friday, and he's paid well. A kind word is all the thanks he hopes for, miss."

Clarice just nodded, gave the bright kitchen a last glance, and hurried out. She'd seen bread, found the ice box, and saw jars of cookies and baskets of fruit. If Milo was hungry, he wouldn't be by the time she decided to grab a late-night snack. *And he'll love that cake.*

She crept to the front door and peered out. Holmes stood out front, talking to a couple of tough-looking men. One might have been one of the fellows who came into the factory with Milo sometimes. She couldn't be sure.

Holmes seemed to be arguing, and the men advanced. To her surprise, he didn't back down. Instead, he pushed one guy out of the way and opened the back door of the car. Seconds ticked past as both men examined the inside of the car. They said something, and Holmes laughed.

After that, he seemed to ignore them in favor of pulling her suitcase and a couple of boxes from the back seat. But when he set the suitcase down next to the front door, he saw her peering out and shook his head once before turning back to the men.

"Gentlemen," he began as he moved away. Clarice couldn't be certain of everything he said, but it became obvious. They could leave or he'd call the police and have them escorted off. What she *did* hear was a strong, bold, "If you wish to speak to Miss Stahl, perhaps you will show the courtesy of allowing her a day or two to grieve and visit her at the factory instead of bothering her at her home."

She watched, her mind swirling with questions as he

retrieved another box from the trunk—when had she accumulated so much stuff?—and climbed the steps again. He fumbled with the handle, and it was only after he'd opened the door that she realized he had done it to warn her.

Once inside, he pushed it shut behind him and gave her a concerned look. "I'll retrieve the rest. Don't get in sight of the front door. In fact..." He pointed to a nearby door. "If you don't mind..."

Even as she stepped into the small space—not quite a closet, not large enough for a room—Clarice had the unexpected thought that Holmes might not be what he seemed. *Is —or was—he a bodyguard, too?*

Voices in the foyer set her shaking. How close she'd come to being discovered. Would they be rough? Demanding? Kidnap her? She didn't know. But what Clarice was certain of is that she did not want to find out.

"Now that you've been so helpful, gentlemen, I must be ungracious and insist that you leave. The family has retired for the night, and I would not wish to wake them. As I said, the factory is the place for Mr. Topo to conduct business with the owner of Meyer's Toys. Her home should be her refuge."

"She'd better be there on Friday," one of the men said.

Holmes cleared his throat. "She will be, and she will not be unprotected."

The words hung heavy in the space between rooms and in her heart. This man couldn't fight against Topo's men and win. She'd have to do something. But what?

The front door shut, and Clarice waited for him to let her out, but she heard nothing. An hour must have passed before she heard footfalls coming, or perhaps it was only a minute. Holmes opened the door with the sort of flourish expected of an English butler in one of those enormous manor houses she'd read about as a girl.

"The coast, as they say, Miss Stahl, is clear."

"Who—?"

"I'll send a note to Mr. Topo. This was in poor taste, and as much as I don't like the man, he's usually scrupulously courteous. He'll apologize on Friday."

Why should I care if a criminal apologizes? I want him to promise to leave me alone—to leave Milo alone.

Holmes hefted her suitcase and a box. "I'll just take these up. You might wish to hang your coat before coming upstairs."

What does he know... or suspect?

Though she'd planned to race after him, that plan failed. She'd just picked up one of the smaller boxes when he arrived downstairs again. Holmes plucked it out of her hands and stacked it atop another box. "It isn't easy to climb stairs if you cannot see where you're going."

A snore greeted her at the top of the stairs. Was it her imagination, or did Holmes stiffen? He passed the door doing a pathetic job of keeping in the snores and shook his head. At the door to her room, he gestured her inside before following her in and setting down the boxes.

He pointed to a twist lock above the knob. "Use it, Miss Stahl. It's important that you use it. Goodnight." And before she could thank him for his help or think of a question for him, he was gone.

Clarice closed the door and turned to examine the room. It wasn't nearly as large as she'd expected, although why she'd expected something the size of a ballroom, she didn't know. It held a large four-poster bed, an elegant but small wardrobe with attached drawers, and a smart, if old-fashioned, dressing table. A small desk and chair sat before a window, and next to it, an armchair and hassock.

Mrs. Grueber hadn't misspoken. Even in the lamplight of the room, the walls glowed warm and golden. It had a fresh richness that hinted at perfect incongruity. It looked well, despite not making sense.

Clarice knelt before her suitcase and opened it. It held

brush, comb, and hand mirror. The few toiletries she used had been stashed inside, as well as shoes wrapped in newspaper. Beneath it all, her dressing gown, shabby as it was. The smaller box contained underthings and her nightdress. She'd start there with the promised bath. By the time she'd finished, surely Mrs. Grueber would be in bed.

FOURTEEN

The night air bit deeper and deeper as he waited for whatever Clarice would decide to do for him. He rose from his crouched position, paced, stretched, and tried not to stamp about when his feet ached for the warmth. He'd just made a pass by the kitchen door when it opened.

Milo flattened himself against the wall and slowly sank to the ground. He'd be wet, but he couldn't be seen. A woman in a thick sweater and no hat emerged. She pulled the door shut and locked it behind her. Milo would have sworn if it would have done him any good.

A twig cracked. It wasn't him, and by the way the woman looked about her, it hadn't been her, either. "Who's there?" she asked.

"Just me, Mrs. Grueber," said a voice he didn't know.

"Oh, Holmes, you'll be the death of me. I thought I'd be murdered before I reached my own door. What are you doing out here?"

"Just thought I'd walk you home. Topo's goons were here a bit ago, asking about Miss Clarice."

His hackles rose as high as Mrs. Grueber's scaling voice. "What? That man has some nerve!"

"I doubt he knows they went this far, but he will on Friday. I'll see to that."

Milo exhaled when the woman asked, "Did our girl manage to avoid them?"

"She did. She's tucked away upstairs—going to take a bath, I suspect. She had that peaked look about her, poor thing. I want to treat her like a child, but she's not, is she?"

Not on your life.

"Don't think she's too far your junior, if I recall correctly. Twenty-seven? Six?"

"Nearly ten years!" Crunching footfalls and distance made the exclamation sound less exuberant than the man probably meant it to be

If Milo didn't know that you didn't mix staff and "family," he'd have suspected a little matchmaking on Mrs. Grueber's part. *Then again, she's just a factory worker in their minds—or was until she inherited. I've got to get in there and find out how that happened.*

If the man were right, however, she could keep him waiting a while. A bath could take a long time. He shivered and hunkered back down out of the wind's path and waited.

Sooner than expected, the back door opened. Milo strained to listen, but the screech of an owl and the rubbing of tree branches made it difficult to hear. Then a twig snapped again. That sure sounded out clearly in the night.

"Milo?" Soft and low, she spoke again. "Milo? You there?"

He rose, and she started. "Oh, you scared me."

Milo put his finger to his lips and stepped out into the light from the kitchen. He followed her into the still-warm room and closed his eyes, reveling in the warmth. Only when he heard her moving about did he open them and watch.

This was the Clarice he remembered. The way she went to work making him something to eat without him having to ask, the gracefulness of her movements. He'd always loved watching her hands as she painted the doll heads at the table in that one corner room.

With food piled on a plate, she handed him a glass of water and beckoned him to follow. "Shh, though. My cousin —" That stopped her. "What a queer thing to say. Anyway, he's upstairs, ossified and sleeping it off." She had an oddly pleased look about that. "I don't want to wake him. You'd have to hit him, and then I'd have to lie and say I hadn't seen him all night. Too complicated."

The house had everything you might imagine in a mansion its size. Portraits on walls, enormous staircases, rich wallpapers. At the second floor, she started down the hall, hesitated, and turned back to the stairs again. She nodded at them before taking her first steps up.

Where are we going?

At the opposite end of the top floor, she must have found what she sought—a small, narrow set of stairs heading up. The top door proved difficult for her to open, but Milo managed without too much noise. Regardless, she hissed, "Shh…!"

Only with the door shut behind them and curtains drawn away from windows to allow a hint of light from the slivered moon did she speak. "I think we're safe here."

"What is this place?"

"I don't know, but I saw it from the outside when I came earlier. I think maybe some sort of attic… but it's awfully clean if it is one. I thought attics were full of all kinds of old things."

She shuffled over to where a small sliver of light spilled in through the window and plopped down, tucking her night-dress and bathrobe under her ankles. "You should eat."

He should not look at her, Milo decided. Unfortunately, he decided it too late. His father had often spoken of how the moon makes everything more beautiful, and it was certainly true of Clarice Stahl. Where her mouth might look too large or her eyes be set a little too wide in daylight or artificial light, here in the moonlight, one thing became certain. There'd never been a more beautiful woman than Clarice.

"Sit. My cold plate is getting lukewarm."

The teasing in her tone should have put him at his ease. He sat, he ate, he even murmured appreciation, but he did not converse. Clarice didn't seem to notice. She told him about her extraordinary day.

"He was my uncle!" she repeated for at least the fourth or fifth time. "I haven't looked for photographs yet. But I was thinking about it on my way to find you, and Dietrich Meyer was a cautious man. He wouldn't pay good money only to accept the first conclusion someone came to. He had to have been convinced."

Milo made a murmur of agreement and continued chewing.

"Oh, and Mr. Topo's men were here tonight. They sounded like they were threatening Holmes if he wouldn't bring me out to see them. Why do they want to see me?"

He took a drink of the water she'd given him and refused to look at her. That helped. Some. "They wanna be assured that their order will be finished before the deadline."

"Why such a late deadline? Stores will have stopped selling such large, garish decor by the end of next week."

Could she really have no idea of what the nutcrackers were for? To test that theory, he said, "What did you smell that night in Meyer's office?"

"Alcohol—probably whiskey since it smelled a little like Mrs. Thatcher's snifter. It was so much stronger, that I could be wrong, though."

He just waited. She stared—he could feel it. His gaze rose to meet hers and his throat went dry at the slow smile that formed on her lips. When she said nothing, his heart hammered in his chest. The smile was for *him*, not for understanding.

The first blink told him she'd begun to work it out. The second was so slow, he thought she might have gotten sleepy. When her eyes opened again, he saw sadness in their depths.

"Mr. Meyer was helping to—run? Is that what they call it? Run alcohol through his business?"

Another swallow of water only helped a little. "H-helping," he croaked out. with a shake of his head. "More-like-coerced."

Again, he watched as she took in his words and arranged them into something that made sense in her mind. "Oh, my…" she whispered. "Oh, my…"

"The chests of the dolls hold sawdust and bottles of whiskey." At her blink, he rushed on again. "S-stores can hell-the-sooch right out in the open that way. He's already shipped out twelve thousand of those things to stores all over the country. He's raking in the dough."

Milo had never seen anything like it. Clarice sat up straighter, her chin jutting out with an imperious flair. She inhaled. Exhaled. Rising to her full height, she blinked down at him and effectively glided to the door.

"I'll return with blankets and a pillow. You can feel around and see if there's a couch or something—an old chaise longue, maybe. But at least you'll be warm, regardless." At the door, she glanced back. "That cake. You're going to love that cake."

Like that, she was gone. A minute turned into three. Three turned into five or maybe more, but she returned, arms laden with bedding that he only saw once she nearly tripped over him. They landed in a heap at his side. "Do you need more water?"

"Is there a bathroom on the floor below us?" At least he managed to keep himself steady for one question.

"I assume so, but I don't know where."

"If I need a drink, I'll fill it in there, and I'll do it at dawn, so I don't hafta turn on a light to find something." She'd stepped back and into that thin beam of moonlight, and his breath caught. "Thank you."

Clarice just walked away, but at the door she seemed to pause. "I'll bring you up something to eat tomorrow. Oh…" Footsteps again. She stood in the light and scanned the area before finding where he'd stashed the plate out of the way. "I'd better return this to the kitchen."

"Maybe grab an apple or a piece of cheese for the attic *topo*?"

"You're not like him!"

That made no sense. "Who?"

"Mr. Topo!"

It cut him to realize that he was just like Mario Topo, but he'd worry about that later. He rose to his feet and followed her to the door as he explained. "*Topo*. It means mouse. I'm the attic mouse."

FIFTEEN

One piece after another began connecting in her mind. She enjoyed jigsaw puzzles of an evening, and that thought brought a pang to her heart. Had Holmes returned all the pieces of her nearly-complete mother and child to the box?

The murder of Mr. Meyer—that is, Uncle Dietrich—reminded her of one of those puzzles. A few scattered wooden pieces. Some fit together to make a picture—the face of a nutcracker attaching to a barrel-chested Russian-looking soldier doll. Others didn't. Peppermint. A moved body.

She needed help, and as irritated as she still was with him, Clarice only trusted one person aside from Milo, and *he* wouldn't trust anyone. *Time's running out*, she reminded herself as she dashed down the drive, her shoes crunching on the gravel with each step.

There was a new telephone box near her boarding house, but where there might be something like that near… no, she couldn't call the house Fortuna. *Maybe "The Elms." All these trees.*

A small piece of her wanted to call from the warm,

comfort of the house, but instinct nixed that idea. She couldn't afford to risk someone overhearing.

Though she'd grabbed more money from the drawer in Uncle Dietrich's desk, they were dollars—silver and paper—as well as a five and a ten-dollar-bill. She'd need two cents for a telephone booth, and even her purse had yielded only nickels, a couple of quarters, and three dimes.

The trolley had long-since stopped for the night. The wind whipped at her, freezing her and making her reconsider the impetuous flight into the cold, night air. Why hadn't she waited until tomorrow? Why not ask Holmes to drive her? No, that would have been a thoughtless idea.

I'll learn to drive the car myself. Imagining herself behind the wheel of the large Duesenberg made her reconsider that. *I could buy a small Packard roadster. They're jaunty little things. Then I wouldn't need to pay Holmes—but no, that wouldn't be right. I couldn't take away the man's income, and what if I need his protection?*

Just at the edge of downtown, Clarice saw a taxi pulling up to a curb. A man got out. "Hey! Sir! Will you ask him to wait for me?"

The man looked her way and hesitated before leaning into the car. He waited for her and nodded as she climbed into the backseat. "Have a pleasant ride home, miss."

"Thank you!" Clarice smiled at the man as she settled in, but the moment the door closed, she turned to see a scowling face glowering at her. "I don't drive fancy women—"

"I need to go to the nearest police station to The Chester-field, please. Do you know which one that would be? I think it's on Grant."

"I know the one." He still scowled. "What do you want the police for?"

"I think I have information in a murder investigation." At the man's skeptical look, she added, "I was too afraid to say something over the telephone."

The man, Bruce, had all sorts of questions. Who had been

killed, how had she found out about it, and why didn't she wait until morning? The first two, she insisted she wasn't supposed to say, but the latter she sighed and said, "I don't know. I just *have* to tell Detective Doyle."

Perhaps he had run out of questions, or maybe he just decided that she must be telling the truth, but the car drew silent but for the rumble of the engine over city streets. They passed The Chesterfield, and at the police station, the driver pulled up quickly. "That's a dollar fifteen, miss."

She handed over two dollars and waited for change. He passed her three quarters and a dime. After a moment's thought, she kept the quarters and left the dime. "Happy Thanksgiving. And thank you for being willing to bring me. I was already so tired."

"You call the depot when you're ready to go. Ask for Bruce. I'll come get you and take you home."

She might just do that.

Her frustrations began anew as the officer at the desk refused to call Detective Doyle and sent for a sergeant. The man appeared looking a little bleary-eyed and tried to be helpful. She had to give him that, but Clarice wouldn't speak to anyone but Detective Doyle.

"I'll call and ask him, miss. How about that? If he says he'll come, he can come. If not, you tell me what this is about. You're wasting police time."

Looks like you could teach me a few lessons in that. Clarice decided that might be antagonistic and stifled the urge to say it. She just smiled, which he took for agreement.

Detective Doyle would come the moment he heard her name. "Who's requesting an audience with his highness?"

I hadn't expected that you could inspire less cooperativeness than you already do. Well done! She just offered her sweetest smile, she hoped, and said, "Please tell him Clarice Stahl is here with information about Dietrich Meyer's murder."

As if magic words in a fairy story, the officer picked up the telephone and placed the call.

Clarice was shown to a chair in the corner of the room and was even provided with a glass of water. The buttons at the desk—that was slang for policeman, wasn't it? She thought so. Regardless, he offered coffee, but she declined. She'd heard horror stories about men's ability to make a palatable cup of coffee. Some things weren't worth the risk.

The minute hand of the wall clock dragged from one to the next. Buttons called someone and spoke low into the receiver, but Clarice didn't hear what he said. It was probably just as well since police business wasn't really hers. Well, except for the murder of Mr.—that is, Uncle Meyer.

Will I ever settle on what to call him? Uncle Dietrich? Uncle Meyer? Mr. Meyer? And what about his brother? What will Karl Meyer think of the sudden infusion of a niece into the family.

That caught her breath. If he were anything like his son, he'd be unhappy about it.

Another glance at the clock showed it clicking on the twelfth minute. It kept swinging from one to the next until the door finally opened at nineteen minutes. *About time.*

Detective Lombardi walked in. The buttons behind the desk—yes, that was definitely the word for a policeman. She had another bit of slang for her arsenal, however Clarice doubted she'd ever have to use it after Mr.—that is, *the* — murderer was caught.

Clarice blinked, trying to recall what had sent her off on that tangent and caught another look between Lombardi and the buttons. *Yes. He definitely sent some silent message, but what?*

"Doyle here yet?"

The officer shook his head. Before Lombardi could speak, the door opened again, and Detective Doyle entered. "What're you doing here, Lombardi?"

"Heard we had news on the Meyer case."

She didn't know what Detective Doyle's expression meant,

but it didn't look good. *Is he upset because he doesn't trust Detective Lombardi or because Lombardi shouldn't trust him?*

Maybe she'd find out now. Regardless, by the thundercloud that threatened to form into a tornado on Doyle's face, Clarice knew things would get worse the moment she started talking.

In the same room she'd been taken to before, Detective Doyle held a chair for her. The sergeant set down her water glass. Lombardi sat down, a pad of paper and pencil in hand. The faintest squeeze to her shoulder hinted that things might be okay. A second look at the detective changed that thought.

Are you warning me? With that question came another. *Because he's not trustworthy or because you aren't?* For just a moment, Clarice regretted not talking to Milo first.

"What brought you in after midnight, Miss Stahl?"

Apparently, Detective Lombardi didn't appreciate being awakened at ungodly hours. Clarice smiled at that thought before remembering that he could see that smile. She tried playing it off as a sympathetic expression. "I'm sorry to bother you, but I think it's important that I confess something."

Of all expressions she might have expected to see on the man's face, confusion wouldn't have made her list. "Confess?"

"Miss Stahl, should we call a lawyer for you?"

"Doyle!"

Ignoring the outburst, the detective elaborated. "It's usually advised—"

"This isn't that sort of confession, but thank you, detective. I appreciate your integrity." Clarice couldn't help shooting a couple of ocular daggers in Lombardi's direction. "When I told you what happened at the factory that night, I left out quite a lot and I deliberately misled you to believe quite a few things."

"Is that so?" Lombardi leaned back, arms over his chest. "Such as?"

"As far as I recall, I didn't lie deliberately. I was very

careful about that because I know that's a crime. But you definitely came to conclusions I wanted you to. I didn't know what to say or do until I knew more." She gave each man a long stare before adding, "Now I think I know enough to be even more scared than I was that night."

Beginning with the sounds of the factory, the cry, the thud, and nearly being knocked down by the man smelling like peppermint, Clarice told both men everything that had happened, right up to when she'd sneaked back into the house and Holmes had hidden her from Topo's men. She told them about Milo's meal and what he'd told her about the nutcrackers.

She didn't mention the attic or that he was asleep there at that moment. She'd lie about that if necessary. "As you can imagine," she concluded, "I am quite nervous about Friday's —um, that is *tomorrow's*—meeting. I cannot knowingly sell these things if they leave my factory..." She swallowed and blinked. "My factory. Isn't that odd?"

Lombardi broke in with a dozen questions of his own. Where was Milo? What made her trust him? Why hadn't she been honest at the beginning? Where was Milo? Who did she think the man had been? Where was Milo? What significance did she give the peppermints? And where... he inserted a few expletives there that nearly got him slugged by Detective Doyle, was Emiliano Natale?

Strictly speaking, she didn't know where Milo was. He could have left. He could be sleeping on one side of the attic or the other. He could be anywhere within a ten-or-twenty-mile radius of the city. But she'd been evasive long enough. If she'd learned one thing from this ordeal, it was that she liked plain speaking and honest dealings.

"I won't tell you where he went. He's not your murderer, and people want him dead. So, you can ask any way you like, I won't answer that. I will ask what to do next, though."

The men exchanged looks, and Lombardi lost his patience. "Listen, girlie, we don't have——"

Detective Doyle interrupted as he stood. "I'll take you home, Miss Stahl."

"You will not!"

An argument ensued. Something in what Detective Lombardi said hinted that he didn't trust Detective Doyle. That detective just stood his ground and refused to budge. Of the two, Clarice decided she preferred the man who didn't swear or shout and informed them that either Detective Doyle could drive her home, for which she'd be grateful, or she'd call a taxi.

Which man's murderous look was worse, Clarice couldn't decide.

SIXTEEN

The house loomed ahead of them—house. Had she gone mad? The place was a mansion—the sort of house large, extended families visited for summer house parties and lived in for generations. It couldn't be more than fifty years old, but it had been designed to look somewhat ageless. With mature trees all about, Clarice could almost imagine that she'd driven into one of the places from an English novel.

Detective Doyle gave a low whistle. "This is yours now?"

"Mr. Hibbard said it is. I find it all very difficult to believe."

The detective turned off the car's motor and turned to face her. "Listen. You did the right thing coming and asking for me. You did. I have a few ideas about tomorrow, and I'll get back to you about them as soon as I find out what is best. In the meantime…" His gaze turned intense, almost stifling. "Don't talk about this with anyone else. Not the guys at the station, not Natale or anyone who works at the factory, and especially not Lombardi."

"You don't trust your partner?"

The man's next words sent a chill through her. "Anymore,

I trust the chief and myself." Was it her imagination, or had
he whispered, "And sometimes I'm not even sure about the
chief" under his breath?

She reached for the door handle, but he started the car
again. Clarice still opened it. "I should walk up the drive. No
one knew I left. If they saw me coming back…"

Doyle reached over and caught her sleeve. "Where's
Natale, Miss Stahl?"

"I won't say. I won't lie to you, but I'm not telling you."
She couldn't risk adding, "And besides, just because I knew
where he was a few hours ago, doesn't mean he's still there."
She just hoped he was… and that he didn't kill her for talking
to the police. She also hoped he liked the part of her idea she
hadn't mentioned to the police yet.

"I could follow you—stay right here until you led me to
him."

"You could, but that would mean you couldn't get me real
help that puts a stop to this."

Where Detective Lombardi would likely have pounded the
steering wheel, Doyle gripped it hard. "You're putting yourself
at risk. You know that."

"I'm at risk regardless, don't you think? At least this way,
my employees…"

He chuckled at her inability to say it without a pause.
"Takes some getting used to?"

"And how!" Clarice chalked that one up to another bit of
slang, but this was one she'd said several times. With slang on
her mind, she stepped from the car and leaned in to say,
"Thank you for the ride, detective, but I think I'd better get a
wiggle on."

His laughter followed her even as the door shut, and she
hurried away. Was it the phrase? Her saying it? Did she
misunderstand how it should be used? *I'll ask Milo.* An inward
wince at his reaction to her evening prompted two more
thoughts. *I'll bring lots of food, and I'll ask that question first.*

A THUD WOKE HIM. Milo jumped to his feet and felt his way to the wall near the door. Footsteps? He couldn't tell. Why would Clarice be coming back, though? It couldn't be her, which meant Topo's men. *They didn't believe her chauffeur. Or...*Could it be that her chauffeur worked for Topo? Not much of a stretch.

The doorknob squeaked a bit as it twisted. In a normal setting, most people wouldn't hear it. To Milo, it sounded like a terrified woman's screech.

Instinct said to jump the moment he saw a shape. Prudence demanded he be sure it was only one person. Whoever it was didn't wear shoes. Must just be one. Clarice or her cousin Martin.

Milo did not want to come across Martin Meyer. That would put a price on his head he'd have to pay with his life. For the second time in recent hours, he prayed. This time for himself.

Near where his blankets were, the figure stopped. He could see her now, carrying a large tray. If he called out, she could drop it. Milo moved with speed and care and grabbed the sides from behind.

Anger fueled him. What was she thinking coming up here like this? "You nearly got yourself choked."

Clarice squeaked, and it was just as well that he'd grabbed the tray. It would have woken at least the house if not the neighborhood. "You scared me!"

How could he explain that creeping up on a man like him guaranteed broken bones or worse? Milo sighed and set the tray on the floor beside the pallet he'd made. "Try to under-stand. I'm serious. I could have killed you."

"I have something to tell you."

At that, she turned to look at him, and when she did, he caught half her profile in the moonlight. All self-possession left him, and with it, his ability to communicate clearly. His throat went dry as he croaked out, "What?"

"I brought more food," she answered with that sort of illogical thought progression that women seemed to have. "Oh, and if I were conversing with someone but needed to get back home, would it be incorrect to thank that person for the ride home and say, 'I need to get a wiggle on,' meaning hurry inside?"

What? The question made no sense.

"I thought it just meant to hurry, but then he laughed and—"

"H-he?" Try as he might, Milo's attempts to keep his voice steady failed him. They said he was dizzy *about* her, but Milo had begun to believe she just made him dizzy.

Clarice knelt to the tray and rose with a cup in hand. "I brought you hot chocolate."

His suspicions grew. This was a distraction. "Tell me."

"I did something you won't like."

Something in the way she said it prompted Milo to reach for his shoes. "What?"

"I told Detective Doyle everything—except where you are," she hastened to add. "I don't think he suspects you're here, either."

Shouting at her wouldn't do any good or he'd have done it. Pounding walls might have been cathartic, but both of those things would have pulled even hungover Martin out of his stupor. "We've got to get out of here."

"No, I don't think so."

Had her brains taken a ride on the midnight train to… wherever that train went? The girl clearly had no idea what she'd done. "They can get a judge and make you tell."

"No, they can't. First, you said Mr. Topo has judges in his pocket."

"And Topo wants me found," Milo said. Strange how when he wanted to shake her senseless, he could speak. "He'd use it." Maybe it was time to make her really see what the danger was. "And now that he may know you were there, he'll want you dead, too."

For an irrational moment, Milo considered asking her to run off with him—maybe to Los Angeles by way of Las Vegas. He'd heard people could get married there with no waiting period. Yes, she had a healthy inheritance she'd be leaving behind, but if she stayed, someone would be reading *her* will in the next few days anyway, so…

Her hand on his arm sent all his more rational thoughts out the window. He covered it with his and squeezed a bit. "You just don't understand." He swallowed hard and rushed through his explanation before words failed him. "How could you? You probably never broke a lingle saw-in-your-life." *Did I get that one right? It sounded backward.*

"I impeded a murder investigation. That's a pretty big one."

Well, maybe it wasn't. He allowed himself a bit of flirting. "Do you know how hard it is for me not to kiss you again right now?"

She blinked at him. Could he blame her? Where had that come from? Then she said the oddest thing. "Again?"

Where he found the words, Milo could only attribute to a subconscious determination to mortify himself. "I almost did to shock you off that fire escape, but when you got back from your interrogation at the police station, I couldn't resist." His voice had dropped to being almost inaudible to himself. "Now it's taking all my self-control not to—"

The way Clarice drew herself up, stiff and quite proper, stopped him cold. She gave him a look that could have been teasing or terrifying. With the shadows playing on her features, Milo couldn't decide which. Her words, however, confused him.

"If you call that continental-style air kiss thing you did a *kiss*, then no wonder you haven't got a—a… *moll*."

He turned the words over in his head, trying to figure out what she meant by a "continental air kiss." Perhaps it hadn't meant as much to her, but he'd relived that moment more than he'd ever admit. It had taken courage to risk offending a girl like her. His chest swelled just thinking of it.

"Outside the wactory falls," he reminded her without even groaning over his mixed words. "When that detective dropped you off. I kissed your cheek and then your—" He swallowed. "I know it was quick, but I did-get the nerve to-kiss-you."

Again, that blinking thing. But then laughter bubbled over. Milo, stunned and not just a little hurt, stared at her before realizing she could be heard. He clapped his hand over her mouth. "Shhh..."

The laughter turned into a gurgle and then a giggle. What she said, he couldn't hear, but she pulled his hand away and said, "It's not a kiss if you never actually touch me, Milo. I'm inexperienced, but even I know that."

She hadn't felt it? How was that even possible?

"I'd kiss you myself to prove it, but this isn't the time or the place."

Milo had to admit that she had a point. He shouldn't be alone with her in the dark in her house. Not like this—not a nice kitten like Clarice. Still, to him it sounded as if she were disappointed at that thought. He'd hold onto that until they were somewhere else, and then he'd kiss her until she couldn't deny it.

I've gone—dead gone on this dame. No. She's not just a dame. This one's a class act, and that's a fact.

"So... all kissing aside..."

Milo heard himself growl and grinned at the bemused look that crossed her face.

Clarice shifted, wrapping her arms around herself. "You are not good for my self-possession tonight. All right, listen. I'm going to call Lily Barnes later today."

"Who?" Did she just roll her eyes at him? Milo had to

stifle a laugh. She looked like an incensed kitten—a live, furry one.

"Lily Barnes. She writes for the Chronicle."

The dame who wrote that article about the murder. Got it. Milo just nodded. It was safer.

"Well, I'm going to ask her to be at the office on Friday morning. I'll send Mr. Dalton off to do other things, and when Mr. Topo arrives, I'll have her get under Dalton's desk. She can take notes and be a witness to everything they say. Then we'll take it to whoever handles prohibition enforcement."

"The IRS." Milo spoke each letter as if with a knife thrust. Criminals with badges. That's what they were. Criminals with badges.

"IRS?"

He repeated it one more time, this time aloud. "Thieves with a badge." Milo spat out the words as if venom.

That earned him a look he didn't think he ever wanted to see her give him again. "Thieves?" Before he could respond, she added, "Wait, they have badges? Like policemen?"

"They have 'em." Milo fought the temptation to swear. "Come in and take a family's only way to make money."

"They're enforcing the law, Milo. It's *their* jobs on the line if they don't."

"All right." She wouldn't look so smug in a moment, but he couldn't resist ensuring she relaxed before he ripped the moralistic rug out from under her. "I'll concede that, if you'll agree that it's thievery when they take that confiscated rum or whiskey and pass it around among themselves or give it to politicians or bribe crime bosses with it."

Stripping her of her ideals didn't feel as good as he'd thought it would. Clarice looked crushed instead of indignant. "Do they really?"

"Yes," he said in a much gentler tone now. "They deally ro." He turned to look out the window and avoid the disillusionment in her eyes. And maybe to hide the heat flooding his face. Deally ro. He'd never live this down if anyone else heard him. "Guys like Topo sell the hooch that people want. They'll get it some way or another. At least his is quality stuff—not gut rot like some bimbos sell."

She moved to his side and stood there, staring out the same window. A soft sigh fooled him into thinking she understood. Her words proved him wrong.

"How noble of him."

"Clarice…"

"We won't agree on this, Milo. You've been very good to me." At that, she smiled up at him. It was a weak smile, but he saw sincerity in it. "You could—probably *should*—have killed me. You might have stopped the real murderer if I hadn't shown up."

In a move he never would have imagined her making, she slipped her hand under his arm and hooked hers around it. Leaning against him, their heads now touching, she added in a whisper so soft he almost didn't hear it. "And you've kept watch over me since then. I know you think I don't know it, but I do."

Was that low rumble *his* chuckle? He felt like a boy with a changing, squeaky voice as he said, "I'm just glad you were paying attention. I was certain you'd get yourself bumped off. You seemed oblivious to everything around you."

"I thought I'd *draw* attention if I were too obvious about it."

The kitten had instincts—good ones. Well, except the honest ones that told the bulls things they didn't need to know. Right. He'd better find out the rest of that plan.

"So, you want the newspaper dame to hide out in the office and take notes—be a witness to what?"

"I'll play dumb and get Mr. Topo to say something about the arrangement. Find out what he plans for us. Tell him I don't want to do any more nutcracker orders, maybe."

"That's a death warrant, and when Martin takes over, he

will do it. Topo expected that cooperation, and Meyer threw a monkey wrench into the cog with you."

His arm went cold as Clarice stepped back, her own arms folded over her chest. "I cannot decide if you just called me a monkey or a wrench."

Before he did something utterly stupid, Milo steered her toward the door. "Let me think on it. Come see me before you call her, though." She'd have protested, but Milo stopped her. "You don't know how these things work. I do. Give me thime to tink." *And find a way out of this mess.* What he'd actually said finally clicked. *And get my tongue in order.*

She gave him a long look. Why, he couldn't decide. He doubted she could see anything so far from the windows. But, at last, she sighed and twisted the knob. "I'll bring you more food after the family leaves."

"See me before they come," he urged. "I'll figure something out."

SEVENTEEN

At the home, Thanksgiving dinners were provided by benefactors who sometimes had odd notions of what orphan children might need for a feast day. Sometimes things were ridiculously lavish, while other years the meal had nearly rivaled that first Thanksgiving the Pilgrims had endured.

As she watched Mrs. Grueber work, Clarice realized the year that those lean, hardly-different-from-any-other-day holidays had ceased. She couldn't give the date, but she knew it had occurred simultaneously with Uncle Dietrich's success in finding her. Did the home still get a good meal?

"Mrs. Grueber, how much do you know about me?"

"You're Mr. Meyer's niece—the one he spent years looking for."

"But he found me," Clarice said. "And yet he never told me."

The woman, probably about the same age as Clarice's mother would have been, dusted flour from her hands, wiped them on her apron, and settled one on each of her cheeks. "He told me the day he found you. I've never seen a man so happy and so sad at the same time. When I asked why he hadn't brought you home, he said, 'It's not safe, Grubby. I have to keep Luisa's little girl safe.'"

Tears pricked her eyes, but Clarice blinked them away. "He sent things to the home, didn't he? Clothes, shoes, blankets, holiday meals…"

As if embarrassed by her gesture, Mrs. Grueber turned back to her work. "Oh my, yes. And toys. If you looked close on any toy in that place, it was sure to have a Meyer's Toys stamp on it."

The question seemed unnecessary, but Clarice felt compelled to ask it. "Will they have a good meal today?"

"Yes, my girl. They surely will. The turkeys are roasting over there now, and Holmes will be taking over the pies and fruit in just a bit." The woman hesitated, put one finger to her lips, and peered through the swinging kitchen door before returning. "Thought I heard something."

Clarice pointed out the window at the sight of a car coming up the drive. "Are they here already?"

But the two women watched as Martin jogged down to meet the car and climbed in. Mrs. Grueber relaxed and set to work. From a crockery roaster on the warming shelf, the woman pulled several thick slices of glazed ham. In a bowl, she mashed a boiled potato with a bit of butter and milk, seasoned it, and covered it with a saucer. Slices of pie, a bit of cranberry sauce, and steamed corn cobs, slathered with butter. With everything settled on a tray, she pulled a dome from the top shelf and covered it. "Take this to wherever you've hidden your friend."

If Clarice had been holding the tray, she'd have dropped it. "Friend?"

The woman shook her head. "Don't try to play me, young lady. I know how much food you've taken out of here, and you'd have to have a tapeworm long enough to reach Louisville for you to have eaten it all. I have three small plates, one large one, two forks, a mug, and a short tumbler missing as well."

Clarice gripped the table in front of her, willing her head to quit spinning. Her head did not comply. Mrs. Grueber grabbed a cloth, wet it, and sponged her neck until Clarice managed to regain her composure. "I—"

"This is your house, Miss Stahl. We work for you. That means we know what we know, and we say nothing to anyone. If you want to hide a whole army of orphans in the tool shed, just let me know how much extra I need to cook."

Still reeling from the woman's admission, Clarice tried to decide if she should tell Milo or not. He might run. If he ran, he might get caught. But someone knowing meant, if anything became dangerous, others might be able to help. That could be good. Couldn't it?

Carrying the small plates had been easy. This large tray, on the other hand, required a rest on the second and third floors both. When she tried to lift again, her arms failed her. Either she was still too shaken or too tired from the previous night. Then again, Martin was gone.

Clarice dashed up the final, narrow flight of stairs and burst into the attic. "I need help."

"What happened?" Even as he asked, Milo reached for his coat.

"Your tray." She flushed at the confused look he sent her. "It's too heavy. Can you carry it the rest of the way?"

"Is it safe? I saw Martin leave, but—"

"Yes…" After a moment's thought she added, "I think so."

Though he gave her an odd look, Milo said nothing. He followed her, picked up the tray, hefted it as if it weighed nothing, and followed her back to the attic. "I don't know that you need to be up here still," she mused. "I doubt Martin will be back upstairs at all. They only put him in a room because he was…" She hesitated. "Spifficated?"

Milo grinned. "Spiff*li*cated. Or Zozzled. What's got you?

Last night you were getting wiggles on, and today you're spif-flicated."

"Well, after talking to the buttons—or are detectives bulls?"

"Bulls," he said. "Definitely. The Joe behind the counter, he's the buttons."

Though she shouldn't feel giddy about having categorized the police into proper slang categories, Clarice most certainly did. She began setting out his meal as she explained. "The girls at the factory consider me a Mrs. Grundy... or a bluenose, depending on who's talking. We weren't allowed slang at the home, so I just didn't pick it up. But it's kind of fun, isn't it?"

"Never thought of slang being a choice." At her pointed look at the tray, he picked up a fork and knife and began sawing at the ham. It steamed still. "Actually, don't think I've ever thought about slang at all. It's just something you hear and repeat because it's what people say."

In the daylight, he'd found a table and chair that, with some soft maneuvering, he'd managed to arrange with a rug so as not to scrape chair legs across the floor. He glanced around him and saw what looked like another chair under a cloth in the corner. It was a wingback with a sprung spring in the seat. "Well..."

"I'll just use the smaller tray from last night..." Clarice went to retrieve it and one of the blankets. "Then I'll cover it with this and... there."

Clarice sat there, perched on the edge of that chair, waiting for him to give her his verdict. Why, she didn't know. Regardless of his opinion, she'd be finding a way to talk to Lily Barnes before the night was out.

MILO'S HEART sank at the look in Clarice's eyes. He knew at a glance that no matter what he said, she'd do whatever she wanted, and trapped up in an attic, he couldn't do a thing about it. Even if he left and found Lily Barnes and tried to stop the scheme, he couldn't trust that the girl would listen.

He hadn't slept much. All night he'd tossed and turned the idea over in his mind as he tossed and turned on the uncomfortable pallet. The risks were huge. If Topo had his men search the office, they'd find Lily and both women would die. It was that simple. If Lily sneezed, shuffled, or even turned a page in a notebook at the wrong moment, she'd be discovered. If Clarice couldn't keep her gaze from straying to where Lily hid... so many things could go wrong. So many.

For a while, he'd decided he'd turn himself into the IRS— be a witness to Topo's crimes. Confess to his. When he'd been brought into the organization, Milo had been warned that his loyalty came with value and at a price. They'd protect him all they could—unless he betrayed them. Then they'd kill him before the courts had a chance to pronounce him guilty. If he confessed, it might protect her. Then again, it might put a price on her head if Topo decided to use her for leverage.

Despite every reason to the contrary, Clarice was right. It was their only option. "I need to be at your meeting with this Barnes dame," he said. "Can you get her to come here?"

Clarice sat, head resting in her hand, elbow propped on the arm of the chair. She looked like a little girl deciding between playing hopscotch or jump rope, and Milo had the irrational desire to ask which she'd picked most as a child. He suspected hopscotch.

She'd like to be in control.

"I'll go call. Perhaps she can come before the family. If they see her here, she could say she's doing an interview."

Milo turned back to the plate of food and gave it serious attention. "How'd you get hot food up here in daylight?"

"Mrs. Grueber knows you're—well, *someone*, that is—is here. She said she wanted you—that is, that person—fed."

If things could get worse, Milo didn't want to know about it.

As she rose, Clarice put a hand on his shoulder and gazed down at him. He'd have stood, too, but she put pressure on it to keep him down. "She says she, her husband, and Holmes are loyal to me. They'll protect whomever I protect. You're safe here, Milo."

That's what you think. Even you aren't safe here.

EIGHTEEN

Holmes doubled as a butler that evening. While Clarice wandered around the drawing room looking at each painting, each figurine, each piece of furniture, he waited in the foyer, ready to greet and introduce the family as they arrived. Only after she saw his face when he led the group in to meet her did she realize his other role in today's family dinner.

Bodyguard. Holmes wore the title well, and if the looks on the others' faces were of any consequence, they knew it.

"Miss Stahl, may I present Karl and Helen Meyer, Martin Meyer, Louise Meyer, and Fredrick Meyer?"

At each name, he indicated the appropriate personage, as if it weren't obvious, and something in his tone told her his opinion of that person. Karl—unremarkable and harmless. Helen… was it concerning or just ambitious? Clarice couldn't tell. The warning note with Martin's name overshadowed even Milo's obvious dislike and distrust. Louise Meyer received the warmest introduction, and the young boy, Fredrick came with a different sort of warning. Clarice suspected he was fond of pranks.

And I am familiar with those, at least.

Louise broke away from the rest first, flinging her arms about Clarice. "I couldn't believe it when Father told me about you! A cousin! I always wanted a cousin." At the merest hint of a clearing of her mother's voice, Louise amended that. "Well, I have them, of course. Mother has heaps of siblings, and they all have even greater heaps of children. But they're stuffy old things, even the little ones. Always so superior. You're the cat's pajamas! I can tell!"

"Louise, really! Don't be vulgar."

Clarice managed to extricate her hands from Louise's in order to greet the others, but as she moved forward, she said, "I'm happy to have a cousin as well. I never knew I had family."

Uncle Karl took both of her hands in his, gazed into her eyes, and nodded. Only a small smile formed, but it looked sincere. "You look very much like your mother—and mine." He turned to his wife. "We won't need to do our own investigation. Dietrich did this well. She is family."

A chill washed over her as Clarice turned to an obviously disapproving aunt. The woman offered a painted-on smile as she gave Clarice a disconcerting once-over. Though she said, "We are so pleased to learn of your discovery," her expression dismissed Clarice as not worthy of notice. It was the simple dress, her unfashionable hair. Clarice had never chosen to afford to keep it bobbed. She kept it knotted at the nape of her neck and left it there except in her own rooms at the boarding house. A pause at her shoes caused the biggest sniff of disapproval, something Clarice couldn't help. She hadn't had a chance to replace them, though she had managed to scrub off most of the paint.

Martin was a surprise, however. That young man stepped forward and clasped her hand with a firm but gentle grip. "I was beastly rude yesterday—was set drunk by friends and— well, no matter. I hope you'll forgive me. Won't happen again."

"Of course, Martin. You've always been kind to me. I've appreciated it."

"All those times I saw you with Uncle Dietrich, neither of us knew we were cousins. Now I know why he told me not to get too friendly, eh?"

Clarice tried to laugh off the joke like the rest of the family, but perhaps she really was a bluenosed Mrs. Grundy. She didn't find it amusing at all. Instead, she turned to Fredrick and said, "I'm guessing you're about... eleven."

The boy grinned. "For another week."

"Well, a guess is a guess," she countered. "I also suspect you like climbing trees and cars."

That earned her a wide-eyed stare and a silent demand for an explanation. But before she could point out the bits of bark on the boy's knickerbockers and the grease under one thumbnail, Louise did it for her. "She's just observant, Freddy. A real smart cracker, this one. I like her."

At least someone in the family did.

Holmes brought in a tall coffee pot on a tea trolley and poured mulled cider for all. "Mrs. Grueber says dinner will be served in fifteen minutes." He lifted a dome off a small tray to reveal tiny pastry cups with what looked to be a savory filling. "Salmon mousse cups," he whispered to her as he slid one onto the first plate.

"They smell delicious. Make sure you get one." Clarice kept her voice low, but her eyes sought his—searching for some hint of how she was doing with this meeting. His smile told her all was well.

For now.

Louise fired questions at her faster than a tommy gun. What had her mother been like? Was living in an orphanage "just awful?" When had she gone to work for Uncle Dietrich? Had she ever guessed he was family? Did she have a boyfriend? Who did she think killed their uncle?

That question got her a sharp reprimand from her mother

and a sorrowful look from her father. "Freddy" stared point-edly at her and said, "Did you kill him?"

Clarice blanched and the rest of the Meyers all began talking and scolding at once. A glance at Holmes showed him amused but watchful. *You're listening. Interesting.*

"I apologize for Fredrick's rudeness," Aunt Helen said. "He will, of course, apologize as well."

"But I'm not sorry. I want to know."

A chill ran over her as Clarice realized Martin paid closer attention to the conversation than he wanted anyone to think. Though risky, she decided to be completely candid. "I didn't, but I think I saw who did—of a fashion." Unexpected emotion nearly choked her.

"How?" The question exploded from Martin and was voiced by Freddy at the same time.

Clarice began telling the story—the *real* story of what happened. Though she tried to keep an eye on everyone at once, it was impossible. As she finished, she addressed Freddy directly. "I lied to the police. Not in so many words, but I left out enough that the story they heard wasn't the truth. Let me tell you, I'll never do *that* again. I could have been arrested!"

From the corner of her eye, she saw Martin watching her. A glance at Holmes showed him watching Martin. At least, she thought that's what he was doing. Aunt Helen suggested, quite stiffly, that they put unpleasant talks aside. "This is supposed to be a somewhat happy occasion. We're all sorry to lose Dietrich, of course."

That seemed tacked on for courtesy's sake. Clarice suspected that Aunt Helen and Uncle Dietrich didn't get on well. Uncle Karl seconded the motion, but the three children overruled the parents three to two. Freddy wanted to know about the tommy guns. Louise wanted to know if Milo were handsome and dashing.

"I think a man like that sounds so dashing. Is he in love with you?"

"I hardly think so. I don't know him," Clarice insisted. "But he saved my life. I owe him that."

"Where'd he go?" This came from Martin, and behind her, Clarice could almost feel Holmes stiffen.

"He didn't tell me." That was true enough—he hadn't told Clarice when he'd left her at her boarding house, and *she'd* told him where he'd go after she found him. "I saw in the papers that some thought he went to Bloomington, but I don't believe it." There. That was also true.

Martin waved his glass at Holmes as if at a party needing more champagne or something. "He obviously killed Uncle."

"I don't think he did." Clarice addressed Martin with as much boldness as she dared. "I believe it was the man who smelled of peppermints. If Emiliano Natale had killed Uncle Dietrich, for reasons that make no sense at all, he would have killed me when I entered that office. He'd have to in order to keep me silent. And, if he'd killed Uncle Dietrich," she added as a new thought occurred to her, "no one would have been there to try to find him and kill him just moments later. No," she continued, "whoever killed Uncle Dietrich ran downstairs, nearly knocked me over, and went for help."

Louise asked the question that had been forming in her mind. "Why didn't that man kill you when he rushed past you? He could have pushed you down the stairs, couldn't he?"

"I probably wouldn't have died," Clarice said after thinking a moment. "I was only five or six steps up. But it would have made it easy to kill me. I suspect he didn't expect me there and got muddled. The murderer hit Uncle Dietrich over the head with one of those awful nutcrackers. But when he ran away, he had nothing to hit me with." It made some sense, anyway. She'd have to think more about this.

Martin just scoffed. "I still say The Nutcracker did it."

"That isn't funny, Martin."

"No, Mother. Natale. That's what they call him. The

Nutcracker, because he squeezes Topo's people until they crack."

Either fifteen minutes had passed, or Holmes had endured all he could stand. Just as Aunt Helen began a tirade against the ridiculousness of modern slang and nicknames, he announced, "Dinner is served in the dining room."

"Good," she said with a snap to the word. "And I trust our holiday meal will not be served with more murder on the side? It was quite enough as a de-appetizer."

NINETEEN

I t was crazy—dangerous, even—but Milo hung about anywhere he could, listening to the family's conversation and trying to get a feel for each person. He liked Louise. Something about her reminded him of Clarice—perhaps the Clarice who would have been if she hadn't had so much difficulty and loss in her life. Freddy was all right. He'd be a better man than his brother for certain. Karl was weak and aloof but kind, too. Helen and Martin, however…

He expected to inherit. He'd have made lots more dough if he had. Unlike Meyer, Martin would have cooperated with anything Topo wanted.

There were rumors among Topo's men that Martin had already made an offer to run other businesses through Meyer's Toys, even while Meyer was alive. Topo would never agree, though. He'd order a hit on Meyer or wait. So far, he'd waited, but had he gotten impatient?

Or worse, had Meyer gotten impatient about Clarice? Said or did something? Would one of the torpedoes have been sent to deal with the problem?

It made sense. Clarice feigned a headache when the meal had ended and asked to be excused. The others left, of course, and Milo came to stand beside her as she watched the car leave.

"How'd it go? I only heard snatches, but I think I have a feel for everyone."

She jumped and might have knocked her head against the window frame if he hadn't caught her elbow. "You startled me!" She rubbed her temple. "I think I need to see if Grubby has aspirin somewhere."

"Not a lie about the headache, then?"

She shook her head. "It isn't bad, but at the first bit of pressure, I used it. I wanted to come tell you what I'd learned." Again, she rubbed. "I should've known you'd be listening."

They entered the dining room just as Grubby appeared to clear away the dessert dishes. "Leave mine, Mrs. Grueber. I wanted it, but I would like some aspirin first. Would we have some?"

"There's a bottle of tablets in the kitchen. I'll just fetch them." She continued clearing as she addressed Milo. "There's a plate for you, sir, too."

"Thank you."

"Mrs. Grueber, this is Mr. Emiliano Natale. You may have seen his name in the papers as 'The Nutcracker.' He did *not* kill Uncle Dietrich."

A voice behind them said, "That's certain."

Milo's fists balled, and he shifted to be able to see the man in his peripheral vision. Clarice smiled, though, and began more introductions. "Holmes, I'd like you and Milo to meet. Both of you are doing a fine job of keeping me alive."

Holmes nodded. Milo echoed the silent greeting. Clarice just shrugged. "Men. Such strange creatures. Anyway, Milo, what do you think of having Holmes sit in on our discussion with Miss Barnes."

What could he say? Milo didn't want the discussion at all, but something had to be done before Topo had time to find and kill either one of them. "Maybe he can talk you out of the crazy idea and into something safer," Milo said.

"Not a chance. Be right back with your food and my tablets."

Holmes looked ready to bolt after her, but Milo wanted a word. "Can we keep her safe?"

Holmes considered the question. "That depends on what idea she has."

"It's risky, but so is stepping outside the door. And something about that Martin makes me wonder if this house is safe."

"He's running with rough crowds." Holmes gripped the back of the chair and met Milo's gaze. "Mr. Meyer knew it and was concerned. I've brought him home singing drunk enough to know he has plans for the factory that meant he'd never have inherited."

That fit with the little Milo knew. But what did it mean? Would Martin Meyer go as far to kill his own uncle? The man had a healthy inheritance already. Property, stocks, even a "summer cottage" in Wisconsin somewhere.

"Would he…?" Milo began.

Holmes shrugged. "He's not an evil young fellow—just a weak one. He likes being admired and considered important. If he got himself in too deep, he might not have had a choice."

"We'll hafta ask Clarice if the man could have been him."

"Could have been whom?"

Both men turned to stare at her, and Milo jumped to relieve her of the tray she carried. After all, it was his meal. "Martin," he answered as he set it at the end of the table nearest them. "Could he be the man who almost knocked you over?"

As she began setting a place for him, Clarice's forehead scrunched into furrows that came to a slight peak over her forehead. He'd never seen anything like it.

"Maybe. It's hard because I was going up and he was coming down. We never just stood side by side, but I am fairly certain he was taller than I am, as Martin is." Clarice gestured for him to sit and eat while she took a chair where the abandoned dessert had been left. "I've been wondering, though. Do you think it could be Mr. Dalton?"

"Dalton?" This from Holmes. "Why him?"

"The peppermints. They were on his desk, and he was arranging a meeting for me with Mr. Topo tomorrow. He sounded awfully panicked about it." After spearing a piece of cake, she addressed Milo. "What do you think? Has anyone ever mentioned him as… um… what would you call it? Cooperative?"

Not that he knew of, but that meant nothing. "Don't know. My area of expertise is those who aren't cooperative."

Clarice's wince sliced right through him. "I suppose that makes sense."

"Shall I go ring Miss Barnes?" Holmes had moved a bit nearer to the door.

"Please. And thank you." That settled, Clarice tapped the table. "Eat while we wait. We don't want to have to rehash everything when she gets here."

The young reporter must have been waiting for their call, because by the time Milo had finished eating and everything had been cleared away, the doorbell rang. Holmes went to answer it while Clarice went to retrieve paper and pencils for everyone.

Lily Barnes arrived in a "Sunday dress" and hat, a leather folio in one hand. He'd heard of her as wearing trousers, a tailored shirt, suspenders, and even a vest on occasion. Her hair hadn't been shingled, but she wore it short in a sort of China doll style.

She's a Sheba, but she really shouldn't be. Clarice is prettier, but this doll's got something.

The reporter took one look at him and nearly whistled.

She shot Clarice a look and said, "I had almost convinced myself that someone had gotten one over on you." This time she did whistle.

"He didn't do it," Clarice said straight off. "You need to know that."

"I doubt you'd have him sitting in your dining room if he had." The girl accepted the chair Holmes offered and pulled a pad from her folio as she glanced around the room. Milo felt certain she'd have given another low whistle if she hadn't caught herself. "You made out good, didn't you?"

Clarice started to ask what she meant—he could see that —but understanding lit her expression. "It's a bit surreal. I feel like a sort of storybook character who discovers she's a princess after living as a peasant all her life. Is there one like that?"

Milo had no idea. Holmes said nothing, but he looked like he had an opinion. Lily Barnes just laughed. "I'm sure one of those Grimm Germans had one. She had probably been stolen because the king forgot to pay for his new robes or something."

Holmes just smiled.

You're intrigued by her. She's too young for you, though, so forget it. Milo didn't know how old the girl was, but she couldn't be far out of her teens.

Discussion began in earnest. Milo wanted to shoot down every idea the moment it came up, and by the look on Holmes' face, he wasn't alone in that sentiment. Clarice insisted that with Lily's notes about the conversation, and testifying as an eyewitness, the IRS would have a perfect case against Mr. Topo for bootlegging.

"We only need to do that. With Mr. Topo in jail, no one is coming after Milo. The courts might even assume that Mr. Topo was responsible for it at that point."

"I doubt that," Lily said. "and I wouldn't be an eyewitness. I couldn't, for example, pick out Mr. Topo in the courtroom as the man I heard in the office, because I've never spoken to him before."

"But I could. You'd be verifying my claim. And we'd both be identifying his voice!"

"Judges like the accused to be identified. But it's a start. Especially if you can get him to answer to his name or admit who he is. But that's tricky."

Holmes cleared his throat. "Potentially deadly is a better way of putting it, if you don't mind my saying so."

There was one other option, but Milo knew it meant he'd probably go to jail. He'd never killed anyone, but he'd done enough damage to get him some time at hard labor. He started to say something when Lily began asking more questions.

Clarice's answers and her ideas sent his blood from boiling to icy cold. She'd get herself killed for sure. He'd have to do it.

"What about this?" Milo shot a "back me up" look at Holmes and laid out his plan.

Clarice protested, of course. He'd known she would. He hadn't expected a counteroffer, however. "I'll agree under one condition."

Do you really think you have a choice?

Lily asked for Clarice's idea as if unfazed by the obvious attempt to keep him from being implicated in any way.

"We call Detective Doyle over here and get his opinion and help—without Milo in the room, of course."

"Are you insane? It could get back to Topo so fast we'd all be dead!"

Holmes nodded, and even Lily looked skeptical. When Clarice continued to lay out her idea—clever but missing vital information—Milo knew he had to give the reporter information that would ensure every bimbo in the country would look for him. The price on his head would be that high.

"He's got half the police force. You know that, right?"

"Well, I knew he had some, but Mr. Doyle seems—"

"No, he actually has *half*. Probably more than half by now. It's been a few months since I heard Carlo saying that half of every team in the city is Topo's. So, he always knows what's up with any investigation. That means either Doyle or Lombardi is dirty."

Clarice turned white. Lily leaned forward. "Hyperbole or fact?"

"Don't know what hyper—whatever. Don't know what that is, but if Carlo says it, it's probably true."

The room's silence announced what he'd been thinking all along. *This changes everything.* The problem was, it couldn't. Because Clarice was right. They needed to be certain that doing this would get the information to the IRS. Alone, they had maybe a twenty-percent chance. With someone on the police force… fifty, maybe.

"We could take it straight to Chief Thomas," Lily suggested. "He's been working hard to clean up the streets."

All eyes turned to Milo. He shrugged. "As far as I know, Thomas is clean, but he's hard to get to right now. Being clean means he's a target. Topo, Solari, even Turgenev—they all want someone who can be bought."

Lily jabbed her pencil at the paper, and the tip broke. While she pulled out a knife and began sharpening a new tip, she said five words that could ensure the plan's failure or success. He just didn't know which.

"I'll go see Doyle myself."

TWENTY

Clarice and Lily slipped inside the darkened factory while Holmes kept the night watchman distracted. They'd have to be quiet and keep the lights off until daybreak when the watchman left.

A couple of minutes later, Holmes jogged up the stairs and snapped on the light. He winked at the women before grabbing a manila envelope from the desk drawer, filling it with blank papers, and sealing it. With a quick wave, he snapped off the light again, and the women heard him hurrying back down the steps before the door slammed shut with excess force.

"Guess he's out," Lily said in the darkness.

"He sounded different from the man that night." Clarice tried to decide what that difference had been and failed. "I just…"

"When the watchman leaves, we'll recreate it—see if we can figure it out."

She hadn't asked about Detective Doyle while in the car with Holmes, but now Clarice wanted to know. "So, what did the detective say?"

"I don't think he's dirty." Lily kept her voice low, but it

carried well. Clarice wondered if she sang in a choir or had taken speaking lessons. "When I told him what Milo said about Mr. Topo going after half of every team first, I could see a flicker—like so many things suddenly made sense to him. I don't think he would have done that if he were guilty. He'd have known what I was going to say."

That was certainly true. Clarice tried to imagine the detective being deceptive enough to do a double-cross and couldn't. "Do you trust him, then?"

"I do. He doesn't trust us—you, especially."

That stung, but Clarice couldn't blame the man. "I don't think I ever deliberately lied to him, but I did let him think things that weren't true. I still can't decide if it was wrong or not. How could I let the wrong man be arrested in a city full of such corruption? He wouldn't get a fair trial."

The ticking of the clock intruded more and more into their conversation with each second that passed. Funny, she hadn't recalled ever hearing the clock before, but with the noise of the factory, Clarice decided it made enough sense. Lily interrupted her thoughts. "I didn't tell my parents what is going on, and they'd never ask, but I did ask Mother and Father what they thought about lying or evading the truth when a life was at stake."

A pang of jealousy struck Clarice's heart. She'd had a mother once. She'd had a confidant and advisor who would help her think through the vagaries of life. Like half the children in the home, hers had been taken by the Spanish flu. Her mother hadn't succumbed to the illness but to the fatigue of taking care of so many sick people. The doctor had said, "If I could, I'd put Spanish Influenza on the death certificate, because it killed her even if it didn't infect her."

Malnutrition probably had, too. How often had her mama gone without so Clarice could have a little more? Clarice really didn't want to know.

Lily seemed to wait for prompting, so Clarice did the expected and asked, "What did they say?"

"My parents actually disagreed with each other. Mother said she'd found it too easy to slide into deceit and outright lying when she did certain types of detective work. Because of that, she turned down a chance to work with the Pinkertons on a regular basis. Father said that as long as a person could separate one's personal life from a job, if that job required deceit, as with a spy or an undercover detective, then he saw nothing wrong with doing what it took to bring criminals to justice."

"That's where my mind has tried to go, but I think I'm stuck somewhere in the middle," Clarice said after a moment's reflection. "I don't want to be comfortable with evasion or deception."

"Mother added that there was still one circumstance where she most definitely would lie without feeling a bit of remorse—she assumed, anyway. I suspect she'd do it even if she did feel something."

"What's that?"

Lily started to say, but a sound somewhere outside froze both of them. Someone spat out an oath—likely the guard—and all was quiet again. "I'm jumpy and didn't know it. Anyway, Mother said that someone once reminded her that Rahab lied about the spies being in Jericho. She didn't just hide the spies and say they weren't there. She told the soldiers that the spies had gone another way out of the city—deliberately sent them in the wrong direction. Mother said, 'I'd lie without blinking to save a life. It may not be right, but I don't see even the faintest hint of reproach on Rahab for protecting someone's life with a lie. If it's not self-seeking and it's life-giving, I'll lie if evasion won't do the trick."

She went over and over every conversation in her mind and finally said, "I think that's what I did. Even when I outright lied about that mouse, I didn't realize it until I'd said something. It wasn't deliberate, and I did say it might not have been there. A lie still, but I tried." She sighed. "I'm trying to justify, but I think I'd do it again, too."

The sunrise came, and with it a walk-through of the factory floor by the guard. He didn't even come upstairs to check the door before locking up and leaving. The two young women watched him lock the yard gate behind him and stroll up the street, head bent and hands shoved in pockets.

Lily hurried to the door. "Let's test those stairs."

They turned on the light for extra brightness below and hoped it wouldn't show in the dawning morn. Clarice hurried down the steps, and even something about that felt familiar. Still, she waited for Lily's call before rushing up the stairs. The young woman's shoes fell hard on each step and sounded completely different from what Clarice had heard. As she passed, Clarice said, "That's not right. It was… lighter."

They took several rounds up and down until both were winded and perspiring. Back in the office, Clarice sat in Dalton's chair and laid her head on the desk. "I think we're looking for a thin man—maybe short. Someone like Milo but much thinner. Except he was tall. Not short. We need a tallish, thin man."

"I don't suppose you know who among Solari's or Topo's men fits that description…?"

"Nope… but Milo might."

"He's carrying quite the torch, that one."

Grateful for a head down and hiding her flaming face, Clarice just said, "I doubt I'd interest him for long. He's used to… to… *bear cats* and Shebas. I'm an old Mrs. Grundy by comparison."

"Sounds to me like you've got a torch of your own."

That shot her upright in a flash. "I wouldn't dream of losing my head over a man I've hardly known a week. Relationships take time. He won't want that, and we'll go our separate ways after this."

THE RUNNING up and down stairs had driven him crazy. Milo sat crouched where he and Clarice had hidden the night Mr. Meyer had died and listened to it all. A few tarps in the back corner of the storage area would hide him well enough, but the walls were thin, and he could hear everything just fine. It wasn't that he didn't trust the women, but they didn't know what mattered and what didn't. They also couldn't take care of themselves.

Milo checked his gun again and waited. Thin man… it could be several, but none of the footsteps had sounded like anyone he'd ever heard. Then again, had he ever actually paid attention to how different people's footfalls sounded?

He didn't know what to think of Lily Barnes, but the doll had managed to reassure Clarice. With all the reassurance and comments she'd made about truth and deceit, he should have realized how heavy it had been weighing on her. He'd been a sap.

"—Relationships take time. He won't want that, and we'll go our separate ways after this."

That's what you think. I do want that. If I can keep out of prison for the next decade.

"I think he'll surprise you."

Clarice's voice sounded hard as she said, "I'm not cut out to be some mobster's moll. I'm not living a life of crime." He'd have been discouraged if she hadn't added, "No matter how much I might like him."

"He can't go back to that life, Clarice. If Mr. Topo finds him, he'll be dead. If Mr. Solari's men find him, he'll be handed over for some favor or another. It's how these organizations work. He'll have to leave here."

She's right, kitten. She's right. Say you'd come, too.

Was that a sigh he heard? Milo couldn't be sure. A moment later, he could almost hear her sitting up straighter.

It showed in every word as she said, "Maybe if we had time to get to know each other—really know. Maybe if I knew where he stood with the Lord. We won't get that luxury, though. He'll have to leave, and now with the factory, I must stay."

Your uncle said to sell and leave.

"I thought your uncle wanted you to sell out and get away from here."

Good thing I'm not in there. I might have lost my head and kissed you, Miss Barnes!

Before Clarice could reply to that reminder, lights came on down on the factory floor. Milo moved deeper into the shadows and found he could hear better with his ear pressed against the thin wall of Meyer's office. If he could only get inside that office. Once the machinery started up, he'd hear nothing.

"I'm going to head down to the washroom and hang my coat with everyone else's. You hide in Uncle Meyer's office until I send Dalton for that paperwork."

There was his chance. Would Lily give him away? He heard the rat-a-tat-tat of Clarice's shoes on the stairs, and this time he had to admit, there was something familiar in it. Had he heard her that night? Maybe last night when she'd gone up to get the will?

Milo looked around him, and seeing no one coming, slipped around the corner and dashed inside the office. Looking up from a small notebook, Lily grinned at him. "Knew you'd be around somewhere. Hear what you needed to?"

"Thanks. Where can I hide?"

They went into Meyer's workroom and surveyed their options. "Up there," Milo said, pointing to the top of a large, wardrobe-like cabinet. In a darkened room and plastered at the back corner, no one would be likely to see them. "One of us goes up there. I can do it because I don't need to get out, or you can do it and I'll help you down. Just depends on what else we find. I take the least secure place."

Sensibly, Lily didn't argue. But they found a place for her under a draped wheeled cart. It looked boxed in, but she'd be able to get out easily enough. "I'm going up then," Milo said. "You can stay out here until Dalton arrives. No reason to be squished there any longer than necessary."

"I'll probably only do it if Topo and his goons show up before I can get under Dalton's desk." Lily gave his feet a shove as Milo hoisted himself up onto the top of the cabinet. "Do you think Dalton could be the guy? He's on the taller side, thin, and has the peppermints on his desk, so one may presume he eats them."

Perched on top of the cabinet, Milo propped his head on one hand and considered. "That description fits Martin Meyer, too. And a couple of Topo's goons. Solari's too, I bet. I'll try to listen when they leave."

"Me too."

The wait began.

TWENTY-ONE

The heavy footfalls pounded on the stairs with the effectiveness of a death march. Under her breath, Clarice whispered, "I think we're going to die."

A pinch at her ankle told her to gather herself together, or so she assumed. Still, it was a bit steadying. "Thanks."

Two men with hands already in their suit jackets entered almost as one. Their eyes darted about the room. One looked at the other, nodded, and took off for Uncle Dietrich's workroom. He returned seconds later with only a nod to the other. That man said something in Italian. At least, it sounded Italian to her untrained ear. *I wish Milo were here.*

The man who entered looked exactly like the picture she'd once seen in the newspaper. Handsome, although impassive. But he was small—would come only to her chin if she rose to full height. The black beady eyes, the wisp of a mustache... the tiny frame. *I could beat you in an arm wrestle. I'm sure of it.*

Uh, oh. Her inner sarcastic had arrived.

"Mr. Topo?" The way he eyed her left Clarice a bit unsettled, so she rose to her feet and offered her hand. Perhaps it wasn't copacetic, but she liked being taller than... well, her adversary. There wasn't any other way to put it.

The man looked ready to kiss her hand rather than shake it, but at last he took it and held it between both of his for a moment. "Miss Stahl. Dietrich's long-lost niece?"

"So the lawyer tells me."

"And the painter of my nutcrackers, I understand."

He hadn't acknowledged Topo as his name, but *my* nutcrackers. Would that be enough to identify him for the IRS? She didn't know. "I understood they were for you, Mr. Topo. But I didn't understand why you'd want so many."

"I am a man of far-reaching business interests. I came to ensure that the final twenty-five hundred would be delivered by December tenth as originally agreed upon."

Thank goodness Milo wasn't here. He'd have lost his senses at the idea that just presented itself. "Actually, I don't see how we can. I've been the painter, you see. And now I need to learn how to run this place. I can't do both. We will, of course, refund any payment you may have made for them."

That impassive expression turned hard and cold. Impassive must be his kinder, gentler self. *Uh, oh. Mustn't become sarcastic.*

"That will not do. We have a contract, and—"

"May I see the contract? Surely, we have a copy here if you didn't bring it. Would it be filed under Topo or...?" She nearly yelped at the pinch of her ankle.

"The contract is a verbal one, Miss Stahl, and you may not be aware of it, but verbal contracts are legally binding. You *will* have those nutcrackers finished and delivered by six o'clock, December tenth."

Every word the man spoke sat on a paragraph of threats. Clarice watched him, just as unmoving as he was. "You must know that you will not be able to sell Christmas decor so late in the season. Oh, and I should let you know," she rushed to add, "Meyer's Toys will focus *only* on toys in the future. You'll need to find some other company to produce things like this."

"You'll produce what I tell you to, Miss Stahl."

You sure like to use my name. I wonder how you'd feel if I threw Topo into every sentence.

"I'm afraid that's just not poss—"

The man on Topo's right stepped forward. "You will show respect. If Mr. Topo says you'll make the dolls, you'll make—"

"Carlo…" Mr. Topo touched the man's sleeve, and Carlo drew back again. "The girl is new, but she will learn."

In an attempt to steady herself, Clarice took her seat, folded her hands on the desk, and gestured for Mr. Topo to sit. And he did. Clarice tried not to gape. Keeping her voice as steady as she could, she met and held his gaze. "I am certain you don't mean to, but that sounded very much like a threat. I'd like to be contradicted in my assumption, please."

Did that make any sense? I don't know. Please let me sound firm and logical.

"You're more intelligent than I gave you credit for. We understand each other, then."

You didn't admit it… even as you did. Now what?

The pinch came to her ankle again. This time, she felt certain it said, "Agree and let them go."

Clarice would do no such thing. "What would my uncle say if he knew his business associate had come into his factory and threatened his niece? I wonder what the police would say." She reached for the telephone. The pinch came hard enough that she nearly kicked Lily.

"I think they would need to inspect the contents of the crates holding these nutcrackers and would find enough evidence to convict you of several crimes, Miss Stahl. Please, don't insult me with idle threats."

She had to play dumb. How… Wide eyes, yes. Mouth agape. Yes… Rising from the chair… small kick to the pinching fingers. "Mr. Topo! If you are accusing me of doing something illegal, state your case now. Call the police. I have just inherited this place, and if it has illegal activity going on, I'd like it stopped just as swiftly as the police would. Perhaps I should call the detectives searching for my uncle's murderer. Detective Lombardi would be interested to hear of this accusation, surely. Detective Doyle most certainly would!"

It worked. The man's face turned bemused at Lombardi and red at Doyle. *We have it right.*

"You'll lay dead on the floor before you can be connected if you touch that telephone." His sneer unsettled her more than the anger or the gun now pointed at her. "Sit down, Miss Stahl."

She sat.

"You will have the dolls ready on the date agreed upon. Do you understand?"

She shook her head. "If there is anything illegal going on with those nutcrackers, I cannot in good—"

"And yet, you have a new family, Miss Stahl. Your cousin is very pretty, isn't she? Named after your mother, I assume? I'm sure your entire family would like to keep her safe and whole, don't you think?"

Was it a threat? Enough? Or was it too ambiguous? Clarice just didn't know. This time a poke at her ankle hinted to push a bit more.

"I would hate to see anyone hurt—my family or any of your men, but again, if this is an issue of law…" She put up her hands. "I am a woman of faith, Mr. Topo. I answer to the Lord Himself." Clarice rose again. "How about a compromise?"

This seemed to amuse the man. His head turned to one side just a bit as he said, "Such as?"

"If there is anything in this factory belonging to you—anything illegal, that is—I ask that you have it removed by the end of today. As a show of good faith, I and another of our girls will work together to finish your order by the agreed date. This allows the company to keep its word without me feeling under obligation to notify the police that there may be some sort of contraband hidden here." She reached for a peppermint to soothe her dry throat. "Will that suit you, Mr. Topo?"

The hard look on his face told her he'd say no. However, after a few long seconds he nodded once. Just nodded. As he turned to go, he said, "You will come with the order on the tenth. I'll have payment ready. My trucks will arrive just after the factory closes. Will that do?"

"Yes."

"Know this, Miss Stahl. Only you and Mr. Gaines should be here when my men arrive."

He'd just stepped through the door when Clarice thought of something. "Mr. Topo." He turned.

"Yes?"

Oh, thank goodness. Confirmation. Clarice tried not to look as terrified as she felt as she asked, "Did you kill my uncle?"

Laughter boomed—much louder than she'd have imagined from such a small man. "No, Miss Stahl. I did not—nor did any of my men." He stepped back into the room and repeated himself. "Nor did *any* of my men. However, I believe one disloyal man knows who did it. I believe you have the power to find out who that person is. If you want to be released from all future business with me, bring him with you on the tenth."

This time, she waited for him to reach the doorway before she asked, "Do you know who did?"

"I suspect…" He only looked over his shoulder as he said, "Look to your family, Miss Stahl. Family usually keeps the secrets."

ANY SECOND NOW, Clarice, and probably Lily, would lay dead on the floor. He just knew it. Part of him wanted to climb down, ready to tackle and try to take the men by surprise. The other part knew that if he made a single sound, he'd personally remove all doubt from the equation. They *would* all die.

She's lost her mind. Why did we let her do this?

But then a thunder of footfalls clattered down the stairs as the men left. It felt familiar now, and with so many feet, Clarice would hear nothing at all. And they wouldn't hear him if he fell. Milo slipped down from the cabinet and landed with a slight thud.

Clarice flew into the room, hand over her mouth. "What are you doing here?" she hissed.

"Trying to protect you. Who knew I needed a muzzle to do that? Are you crackers?"

Lily huffed. "Completely. She should be black and blue with me trying to shush her, but other than a near kick in the teeth, it got me nowhere."

Clarice ignored both of these jabs and said, "What are we supposed to do with you? Mr. Dalton will be back any minute."

He hadn't considered that.

A small, hissed argument commenced until Lily grabbed each of their shoulders and gave them a shake. "Enough. Clarice, you go down into the employee cloakroom and grab a hat that looks as far from anything you've ever seen him wear but a lot like a bunch of others, too."

"Like a cap?"

"Great. Get that. And where can we find something to use for a razor?"

Milo couldn't imagine what Lily wanted with that. In fact, he was quite certain he didn't want to know. Clarice just stared at her feet for a moment before moving into Meyer's office. "I think he might have a knife…"

From the drawer of the worktable, she pulled out a rather mangled looking safety razor. "Will this do?"

"Even better. Scissors…" Lily reached for them. "Go get that cap. I get to play barber."

Milo went cold.

In seconds, the bulk of his mustache lay in his hand. "If we only had some soap and water." Lily fussed for a moment before sighing. "I'll have to find the employee washroom. If you get all red from scraping, it'll give away our ruse."

"I must look ridiculous."

"You're going to look about ten years younger."

"Exactly why I wear the mustache." Milo felt the razor. "I'll be lucky if this blade has any life left in it."

By the time both women returned, Milo had grown from nervous to terrified. Lily pulled out a compact and handed him a towel while she held the compact up for him. He only nicked himself three times—a blessing as far as he was concerned.

Lily asked about a camera, and Clarice disappeared again. This time, she took so long that Lily and Milo moved to the hiding place—and just in time. Dalton appeared and set to work making calls. When the next set of footsteps sounded on the stairs, Lily peeked out and beckoned Clarice over.

With the cap on his head and a camera slung around his neck, Lily led him through the factory, stopping here and there to have him take a couple of pictures and ask questions before they strolled out into the cold morning air. "Get into the car with Holmes. He can take you back. I'm going to meet Doyle."

And with that, she was gone.

TWENTY-TWO

No one raised more than a curious or excited eyebrow when Lily and Milo walked through the factory floor on their way out. Clarice, remembering all Lily had said about her mother's perspective, kept her explanations factual. Yes, Lily Barnes would be writing an article about the factory. Yes, they'd been talking upstairs. Yes, the man who had come in was Mario Topo. No, Emiliano Natale had not been in on that conversation.

"I need two people to help me," she said when the questions became awkward. "We need to finish up this nutcracker order as soon as possible."

Mary volunteered, as Clarice had expected. To her surprise, Edith did, too. "I'm sick of being cheeky," she said with a saucy wave of the brush. "I'll do the eyes, you do the cheeks, Mary can do the mouths. She gets mouthy sometimes." The other painters snickered.

Clarice would have protested, but there didn't seem to be much point. They all worked eyes for two dolls each. Then Clarice took over with cheeks while Mary kept on with the eyes until Clarice had done three sets of cheeks.

Having prided herself on her work ethic, Clarice now realized she hadn't been giving the project her best from the beginning. She easily doubled her earlier time if not tripled. The chatter around them cycled through topics like the revolving door at Wakefield's Department Store. Mr. Meyer's murder, Clarice's inheritance, the new movie at the Imperial, and the likelihood of Garrison Prince really staying out of Hollywood pictures.

"He was becoming more popular than Rudolph Valentino! Of course, he'll be back!"

"I read in *Photoplay* that he married a cigarillo girl and adopted a kid off the streets. He's in *Bible college* now." Ruth sighed and set down the tiny porcelain hand she'd been painting. "No... I think we've seen the last of the Prince."

"I'm parched," Edith muttered. "It's ages until they let us out of our cells." She flushed and shot a look at Clarice. "Sorry. You know I'm just funning, right?"

It was the first hint that she was no longer "one of the girls." She'd been reassigned to "boss" status, and learning anything from them would be more difficult now. After a few minutes of quiet chatter, the usual joking and teasing began. They finished the cart before Mr. Gaines had returned, so Clarice settled the dolls on it and wheeled them away.

Just as she returned, Edith groaned about being thirsty *and* hungry now. Emily had taken up the lunch cry and spoke of a container of hot soup. "My brother won one of those Thermos things in a rowing contest. He lets me bring hot soups during the week sometimes. It's wonderful."

"I looked into them. Too rich for my blood," Mary said. "But it does sound wonderful. Maybe we could get a hotplate for the cloakroom—cook a stew in there while we work."

All eyes looked at her as Clarice sat down. She shrugged. "I don't know if that would be safe, but I can't see why one can't be set up in Uncle Dietrich's office. If we all brought in something for it every day, it would be ready by lunchtime."

Mary gaped at her. "But Mr. Meyer went to a restaurant most days, didn't he? Won't you do that?"

"I don't know. I can't imagine it. Maybe Holmes took him home for lunch. Mrs. Grueber is a wonderful cook."

Edith stopped mixing paints as the squeaking wheels of the cart brought a new batch of nutcracker dolls. "What will you eat today? Lunch counter with the peasants, or crystal and china at The Chesterfield?"

Clarice hadn't thought about it. "Probably the lunch counter. I didn't think to ask Mrs. Grueber to fix me anything."

As she pulled the first doll toward her, Mary sighed. "I wonder if Mr. Dalton is impervious to flirting."

I wonder that you know the word impervious. You never cease to surprise me.

"—beg for one of his peppermints."

Edith picked up on that. "Oh, that's right. He always smells of peppermint, doesn't he? Think he'd fall for the fainting female routine?"

The discussion turned to how they'd best distract him and who had the best pickpocket skills while Clarice turned Edith's statement over in her mind. *Always smells of peppermint. She'd never noticed it, but someone had. And someone had smelled of peppermint that night.*

Peals of laughter rang out as Ruth did a terrible job of trying to steal Emily's handkerchief from her smock pocket. "We won't send Ruth in!"

"You do better, Miss Edith!"

Mary argued. "We just have to get him out of the office. Then someone can go in and raid his bowl while everyone else is distracted with our fainting Flossie."

Ruth blinked. "Who's Flossie?"

The laughter returned, and Ruth turned a rather unflattering shade of scarlet. Edith turned to Clarice. "Or you could do it. You could ask Mr. Dalton for a few of his peppermints.

He can't turn down the boss, can he? We'd replace them come lunchtime."

Clarice started to demur, but an idea struck her. How would Dalton react if she mentioned peppermints and that she'd smelled them that night? Milo would have kittens over it, but he couldn't hurt her in a factory full of people. Could he? "I'll go see. What could it hurt?"

All the way to the stairs, up the stairs, and to the office, she rehearsed her question. She'd have to time it just right to be out of reach when she mentioned it. Just before entering, she heard him say, "No, Mr. Meyer. There haven't been any changes that I'm aware of. You'll have to take those questions up with the new owner, though. I really shouldn't be talking to you about this."

Clarice stepped into the office with a smile on her lips and questions right behind. Which "Mr. Meyer"? She wouldn't ask, but she wanted to know. "Hello! I'm here on an errand of mercy—that is, I'm here to throw myself on yours, actually."

Dalton disconnected the call and looked up, hands folded and just a bit of a tremor in them. *Because of me or the call?*

"What can I do for you, Miss Stahl?"

She pointed to the bowl of candies. "Might we beg for your candy for a couple of hours? We'll replace them while we're out for lunch." She leaned close. "Normally, I wouldn't ask, but I must finish those nutcrackers for Mr. Topo, and the girls are feeling awkward around me now. I thought it might relieve some of the tension. I'd just need..."

But Mr. Dalton had already reached into a drawer and retrieved a paper bag. "I buy them at Sweitzer's by the pound. It's less expensive that way. My throat goes raw easily, so I keep them handy to soothe it. Take the rest. I'll replace them later."

"Use the office funds for it, Mr. Dalton. Thank you so much." At the door, she caught the jamb with one hand, looked back and flashed what she hoped was a teasing smile.

"You know, I do believe Uncle Dietrich's murderer stole one of your candies. I smelled peppermint on him as he rushed past. If I didn't know you'd already left, I'd think you were guilty!"

Mr. Dalton turned positively green.

ONE LONE LIGHT shone in an upper window just as it had the night Dietrich Meyer had been murdered. The watchman rounded the east corner, whistling "California Here I Come," and Milo slipped through the gate at a run. Only when he reached the fire escape did he pause for breath—and reflection. The watchman. *Where was he that night?*

The longer he sat there, waiting for the man to make it all around the building before working the key into the lock and slipping inside again, the more concerned Milo became. No one questioned the missing guard. Did the bulls even know about him?

Then again, what use was a watchman who just walked but never actually watched anything? He'd consider that later, too. Meanwhile, he had a few choice words for Miss Stahl. Even Holmes was ready to shake her into Sunday.

He crept down the passageway to Meyer's office and listened at the open door. Nothing. A peek into the office showed it empty. Dalton was gone. At the stairs, he recalled Clarice's obsession with the footfalls and clattered down exactly how he thought he would if he'd tried to get away after killing someone. Would it sound right to her?

For one irrational moment, he feared he'd do it so well that she'd be convinced it had been him. *As if I could be upstairs and out the door at the same time.*

The night watchman had switched to "My Buddy" now.

When he stepped into the light at the painters' corner,

Clarice stood there holding a gun with a shaking hand. "Oh! Milo. You scared me." The hand still shook.

Milo reached out and shoved her arm upward before removing the gun from it. "Where'd you get this thing?"

"Dalton had it in his desk. He said I should keep it close if I were staying late." Clarice dropped into a chair. "I had started to think he was guilty, but why would he give me a gun if he were?"

Milo checked the cylinder and sighed—both in frustration and relief. "Maybe because there's no lead in this thing."

"What?" Clarice sank into her chair, her hands shaking worse than a new leaf in a windstorm. "I— Why would he—?"

A sound—soft but distinct—prompted Milo to cover her mouth with his hand. With one finger to his lips, he pulled her up and crept toward the wall where a switch turned lights on and off. He listened. Was that a footfall? Inside or out?

Leaning close he said in a strangled whisper, "When I squeeze your hand, go upstairs and out just like we did that night. Don't look back. Just go. I'll meet you across the way."

A ping somewhere hinted that metal had touched metal. *Dear, God. Please let there only be one, or she'll die.*

With each passing second, his ears became more attuned to every sound. One sound he should have heard he didn't. The night watchman's whistle. *This is an ambush. On a kitten like Clarice. Why?*

Milo whispered, "Keep quiet and get ready" as he slipped his hand into hers. It might be the last thing he said to her, but he couldn't risk more. Instead, he kissed her cheek and prayed she felt it that time. *God, I'm doing an awful lot of praying these days. Consider this one, too.*

A shuffle… it was close. Whoever it was would come around that corner any second now. Milo slid his hand up to the switch, closed his eyes, and listened. His fingers twitched.

He crouched a little, arm still raised to snap off that light… now!

The light went out, he squeezed Clarice's hand and dove toward the sound of movement. An "oof" preceded a string of oaths. Strange, Milo had never minded the colorful language of the men he worked with. Now he wanted to pour lye down the man's throat to clean it out. *Excessive.*

A foot connected with his shoulder. Milo flipped around and landed a punch to the man's jaw just before another kick to his gut rolled him over. He staggered to his feet, ready to dive again, when a gun—*not* the Weebly Clarice had been holding—filled his vision.

"Right there. Just stay right there." The man's thick accent —a blend of Italian and Chicago—told Milo this man had to belong to Solari.

"You the torpedo from the other night?"

A laugh answered him. "If I'd been here, you'd be dead. Still, Topo's going to be happy to hear I've got you for him. He'll pay nicely for that."

Did that mean the bimbo planned to keep him alive to hand over or…? The worst of it was, Milo couldn't decide if he'd rather die here or take his chances with Topo. He might be able to talk Topo into believing he'd gone hiding to find who killed Meyer for *Topo's* sake instead of his own. But if he couldn't, death wouldn't be swift. This guy would make it swift.

"Where's the dame?"

Milo sized up the situation and found it just safe enough to push a bit. "Who killed Meyer?"

"None of your business." The man pointed his gun at the floor near Milo's feet and fired once. "I'll ask again. Where's the dame?"

"Gone. Where's the watchman?"

Two more shots. If one hit a knothole in the floor, it could ricochet. Milo needed to stall—give Clarice enough time that she could be far enough away to make it not worth going after her. That she was only yards away didn't matter. They needed to think she'd gone blocks—to the police, even. There was no guarantee one of Topo's or Solari's men would assist her. Yes...

Three more shots. "Time to dance, sugarplum. Dance and sing."

You're crackers.

Still, despite himself, Milo shifted a bit away from the flying bullets. Two pinged off the floor, but where, he didn't know. A shadow shifted somewhere behind the goon. Milo's heart thudded. *No... no, Clarice I said to go!*

The shadow narrowed and shifted into a silhouette. A gun cocked. Solari's man started to turn, but Detective Doyle said, "Drop the gun, Romano."

Milo saw it but not in time. Two shots rang out in quick succession. Pain seared through his cheek. Romano dropped to the floor. Doyle turned the gun on him. "You'd better be glad I heard that." He pulled a handkerchief from his pocket and thrust it at Milo. "Press that in and sit before you fall. I'll get help."

"No!" Milo struggled to hold on, but his head swam. "Get Clarice out of here."

Doyle looked sick. "She's here? What's she doing here?"

His head swam. He knew Doyle not knowing that meant something, but what. Then Doyle grabbed his shoulder. "Stay with me. Come on. We've got to get you out of here. That handkerchief is soaked through."

TWENTY-THREE

Clarice froze on the last rung of the fire escape. Somewhere near the gate, a man moved. Should she go back up and warn Milo, or would it be better to run for help?

Help, she decided. She couldn't do anything, and getting herself killed wouldn't save Milo, but if he could evade them long enough… Definitely. She dropped the last couple of feet when she heard the footsteps running to the door. A peer around the corner showed the door sliding shut again.

Clarice ran. She'd made it halfway down the block before she heard it. Was that gunfire? She ran faster. At the drugstore two blocks over, she found the owner locking up. "I need the police. Can you call the police? Meyer's factory. Hurry."

The man just blinked at her. Clarice didn't have time for this. She dashed around the counter and lunged for the telephone hanging on the wall. The operator promised to send the police immediately. After half a second of consideration, she asked to be put through to Doyle's station. "Over by The Chesterfield? On Grant?"

The man at the desk promised to let Lombardi know she'd

called. "No! I need to talk to Detective Doyle. It's an emergency."

"Well, he's not here, is he? So, you just go on home, and Lombardi will get to you when he has time."

I'll bet he will. "Never mind. I'll find Doyle myself. Lily Barnes knows how to get ahold of him."

A roar of protest followed, but Clarice just replaced the receiver and promised the shopkeeper that she'd return the next day with a nickel for the calls. Outside the store, she hesitated. Should she call Holmes? Instinct told her she should, but the door locked behind her. After banging a couple of times, she gave up and took to the street at a run. She'd find somewhere else. She needed Holmes.

That thought brought her up short. Holmes. He knew she was there all alone. Did he send Milo… or the other man? And the man on the stairs. Could it have been Holmes?

Her mouth went dry as pieces fit together. Clarice shook herself. No. Holmes had saved her from Topo's men. Why…?

This time, the dry mouth caused her to choke. If he worked for Solari, and *those* men had come, would he have protected her then? Was the man Milo had attacked sent by the rival… gang? That's what they were, wasn't it? A gang? Sent by… Holmes?

She couldn't remember anymore. With no money for a taxi, Clarice kept walking until she found an office with a light on. Babcock's Ltd. A car roared up the street as she began knocking. The squeal of tires stopped her. She glanced over her shoulder and then stared as the car reversed and shot back toward her. The door swung open, and Detective Lombardi called to her. "Get in."

"I—"

"Now, Miss Stahl. There's a report of gunshots at your factory."

Of course, there is. I made the report.

The man probably had a gun. What "bull" didn't? Clarice

slid into the seat next to the detective and pulled the door shut. What should she say? Her head buzzed until sense became more than unlikely. It was now an impossibility.

"Where's Natale, Miss Stahl?"

"I don't know." That was the truth, but the detective's growl told her it wouldn't be sufficient. "He helped me get out of the factory when we heard someone coming in. Then I heard gunshots as I was running away to get help. I went to that drug store…" She pointed as they drove past the now-darkened store, and Lombardi huffed. "Um… and well, I called your station."

"And asked for Doyle." He shot her a glare. "Not kosher, Miss Stahl."

She tried to distract him by playing the dumb Dora. "I've spoken more with him. It was only natural to think of his name first."

Lombardi shot her a look, and after turning the corner onto the street leading to the factory, seemed to relax. "Yeah, well…"

A single light shone in the office upstairs. Had it been on the whole time, or had Milo gone up there? As Lombardi ordered her from the car, swearing about something she couldn't understand, and urged her inside, he said, "Show me."

"Show you what?"

"Where you were when you heard someone come in. Who was it?"

"I didn't recognize him. Actually, I didn't see him. Milo pushed me out of the room when he went to attack the man. I got out, and when I went for help, I heard the gunshots." Her throat constricted. "He could be dead."

"Let's hope." After half a second, he added, "Not."

Had he swallowed hard at the thought of someone dying or tried to hide his true feelings? Clarice couldn't decide. Just inside the door, as Lombardi threw the enormous switch that lit the whole factory floor, Clarice saw it. A spot of blood. Several feet away, she saw another. And another. "Someone's bleeding!"

"With gunshots? Of course, you dimwit. What do you expect?"

*I expect an officer to treat ladies with respect—*citizens *with respect, in fact. Perhaps "bull" is a better name for men like you after all.*

"Come on. Show me."

The closer they drew to the painters' corner, the more blood they found. Either whoever was injured stopped bleeding or they'd managed to staunch it better the closer they'd gotten to the door. She rounded the corner and turned away at the sight of a man crumpled on the floor. A whimper escaped before she could steady herself enough to ask, "Is it Milo?"

"Romano—one of Solari's men. This'll be war." A few more expletives echoed through the building. The man's hand clapped around her arm and held it in a grip sure to bruise. "Where's Natale!"

"I don't know! I told you. I left."

"Out the front?"

Clarice shook. Her hands, shoulders, lips—even her eyelids shook as tears coursed down her face. She couldn't lie. Somehow, he'd know, but she didn't want to remind him about the fire escape. She might need it.

Lombardi jerked her back and forth until her teeth rattled. "Which way did you go?"

"Upstairs." That's when she realized the light to the office had been on as she'd rushed past.

"How'd you—?" He froze, considered something, and pushed her. "Go on. Show me."

Though she tried to wrench away, he still held her arm fast. "Please! You're hurting me. This sort of brutality won't go over well with Chief Thomas."

"You won't be talking to him. Now move."

Twice she slipped as she dashed up the stairs. The detective was right on her heels, ready to shove her upward with his foot to her posterior if that's what it took. She knew because he did. "Ouch!"

"Move!"

That's when she heard it. The odd, ooohhh—ooohhh... of the cranked sirens the police sometimes used. Her mind insisted she knew what it meant, but she couldn't make it unlock that door of information. Detective Lombardi shoved her into the office. "Okay, now how did you get out?"

Her eyes focused on the bowl of peppermints as some kind of anchor. Metal. Thin. Brass? Perhaps. Not well polished, if so. Pewter. That was it. Not golden enough for brass or bronze. The man poked her again and asked where. "Not here," she whispered. Those peppermints...

"Where?"

"At the end of the walkway." Had she answered, or had someone else?

Lombardi pulled a sheet of paper from the typewriter and grabbed a pencil from the desk pad. "Write."

"Write what?"

"Write, 'I killed Dietrich Meyer. I'm sorry.' And sign your name."

Shocked out of her stupor, Clarice refused to take the pencil. "But I didn't!"

Perhaps her subconscious expected it. Maybe she'd been as shocked as she could be by that point. She didn't know. But when the detective pulled out his gun and ordered her to write that note again, Clarice wasn't surprised, and she refused.

"Shoot me, then, but I'm not going to confess to a crime I didn't do." The sirens were louder now. "So just shoot me."

I sound brave enough, but am I? Then again, if I wrote it, what would he do with it?

Lombardi grabbed her with his free hand and shoved her out the door and down the walkway. The barrel of the gun pressed against her neck as he asked, "So how'd you get out of here? The fire escape, right? Where is it?"

"The door—at the end."

Time swirled in a cyclone of thoughts, actions, sights, and sounds. One moment she'd been shoved into the dark walkway. The next, she was out on the fire escape. "Jump."

Clarice turned to stare at the man. The sirens had almost reached them. "What?"

"Jump."

Mind racing, she remembered that first night. If she touched the escape railing, she'd hold on tight. Would he smash her hand to make her let go and push her off? Shoot her? Would she survive a fall like that? The equivalent of three stories, really. People had survived that much, hadn't they? She'd nearly fallen that night…

"Now!"

Still facing him, she took one step back. Then another. Odd, he wasn't moving forward. When she didn't take another step, his pistol raised. There couldn't be much more room. If she weren't careful, she'd fall.

"Just another step, and it'll all be over. Go on. Hurry up now, they're turning into the yard. They'll see. This is perfect. Now!"

When the gun raised again, Clarice realized he wouldn't shoot. He'd throw. She took a big step back and felt herself falling.

All the fuzziness fled as she dropped. Clarice grabbed for the rungs. Her fingers flapped against a few, but she managed to grip one. Pain ripped through her right shoulder, and she let go, but her other hand gripped onto the next rung. That hurt as well, but not nearly as much. Her right arm hung useless. She couldn't work her way down. Not when her arm wouldn't reach for the rung.

Dangling there, her hand cold and losing its grip, she realized she'd never hang on long enough. *Lord, help me!*

Maybe He shouldn't. Had she asked *Him* about her decision to stay late? Had she asked *Him* what to do about the business, about Mr. Topo, and about the little puzzle pieces that now made a fairly clear picture?

A shout below her demanded she hang on. Her hand slipped more. Clarice shuddered as she realized it was a matter of a few seconds before she fell. Several men stood down there and one began to climb. Another. Her hand slipped. She managed to grip three or four rungs down... and to kick the man climbing to reach her. That hand started to slip almost immediately, and her arm burned with the pain of it. *At least I'm not kicking and thrashing. That has to help. I have some self-possession left, anyway.*

"Step onto the rung!"

Her mind fumbled with those words. Step?

A hand gripped her foot and set it on one of the rungs. It repeated it with her other foot. *What an idiot! Why didn't I stand on the rungs?*

She slipped her arm over the rung and allowed her armpit to help hold her steady. The officer climbed up beside her and touched her bad arm. Clarice screamed.

"I'm not going to hurt you!"

"You just did! I grabbed with that arm going down." Tears coursed down her cheeks. *Do you have to be so dramatic?* "It just really hurts, and I can't move it."

"Dislocated, most likely. The doctor'll fix you up." The officer grinned at her. "Strange place to meet a pretty girl, but I'll take it. James Malloy at your service, miss."

"Detective Lombardi. He's in there. He made me jump."

The man's expression could mean anything. Clarice prayed she hadn't just sealed her fate. Then, even in the semi-darkness, she saw his jaw twitch, and he called down, "Lombardi's the double-crosser. He's in the factory!"

Head swimming, Clarice decided she should thank him. Instead, she said, "I think I should sit down."

The man grabbed her about the waist and held fast. "Oh, no you don't. And no slapping me for getting fresh. I'm just trying to keep you from spending Christmas in the hospital."

A black fog filled her, but one more thought emerged. "Is this where I say, 'the bank's closed'?"

The last thing she heard was laughter.

TWENTY-FOUR

P ain. Milo knew he couldn't possibly be dead, because of the pain. If hell were real, he'd be in pain all over, not just from the neck up. *I guess I should thank You for not killing me, eh? Okay, God. Thanks. Now... this pain...*

"I think he lives."

That voice. Milo knew the voice, but he couldn't place it. *Not hers.* Well, the voice was *a* her, but it wasn't *hers.* Would that thought make sense to anyone else? Probably not, but he knew. That's what mattered.

"You're going to have an interesting looking face, Milo. It's a good thing that Clarice appreciates you as a person, or you'd be sunk."

Only one woman would know that Clarice even knew him. Well, except for the cook—whatshername. He tried to speak and failed. The movement of his lips sent a swath of fire across the left side of his face.

"Don't talk." A hand wrapped around his. "Just squeeze if I say something that makes sense."

He squeezed.

"That was easy. Okay, want to know what's going on?"

He squeezed again—harder this time.

"Clarice called the station on Grant. Said she heard gunfire at the factory and told the buttons at the desk that she would call me. Not sure why she told him that, but I know it because I got a call saying that I was under orders *not* to go anywhere near the Meyer's Toys factory. So, of course, I went. Got there in time to see a buttons rescue Clarice from the fire escape. That girl!"

Fire or no fire, Milo forced his eyes open. Only one seemed to work. Doing his best to ignore the pain (and failing), Milo breathed, "What?" through clenched teeth.

"Shh… I'm already breaking every rule and pulling every string known to man. If a nurse finds out you're talking, I'm out of here, and you won't know what happened to our heroine."

Heroine. Of course, Clarice was a heroine. Now, if he only knew what she'd done. He squeezed again.

"She's in the women's ward next to a bunch of recuperating new mothers right now, but she's fine. Just dislocate— well, let me tell you what I've gotten out of her so far. I can tell there's a lot more. I think she's figured out what happened, but they gave her something to help her sleep, and she nodded off before I got it all."

Milo just squeezed to get her to keep talking.

"So, when you pushed her out, she went down the fire escape and ran off. Just as she did, she saw someone we think was Doyle running in. Halfway down the block, she thought she heard gunfire and ran to a drug store where she called the police." Point by point the story unfolded. "She's fixated on peppermints. Says they prove everything. She also asked if Martin Meyer has connections with Solari, if Dalton has connections with Solari, and who hired some girl. I couldn't get her name. Doyle's looking into—"

Doyle's voice broke in saying, "—why you're in this room, Miss Barnes" and drowned out whatever else she'd said.

"I had to see that he was all right—for Clarice. Oh, and so

he'd know what's up." She eyed Doyle, and Milo wondered why until she asked, "What happened with Lombardi?"

Milo squeezed hard. There was something more to this Lombardi thing than him taking her back to the factory. He could hear it in Lily's voice and see it in how Doyle refused to look at him. "Wha—?"

"Shh... You'll get me thrown out."

"You're getting thrown out anyway. I'll take you home or to the Chronicle, or wherever, but you're leaving. We need this man able to testify, and he won't be if he gets an infection from lack of rest or whatever causes them."

The hand slipped from his and Lily bent over to kiss his forehead. What was with—?

"She's all right. She's just fine. Remember that. Bravest girl I know. And she's just fine."

"Let's *go*, Miss Barnes."

"I'm coming!"

Left alone in the room, other things invaded his consciousness. The swish of fabrics and taps of shoes as people moved around on the ward or down hallways. The smell of iodine and... mercurochrome? He couldn't be sure. All very antiseptic and unappealing. He'd rather smell his mama's pasta or his nonna's bread. Ahh... that sounded wonderful.

Turning his head hurt too much, so he closed that eye and tried to remember everything. Holmes had returned without her—livid that she refused to come home. He'd dropped off Milo and promised to return the moment they called. *"I'd stay, but something is happening with Solari's group tonight. I have a friend inside the organization. He'll tell me if I can get over there. Can you keep her safe?"*

Milo winced at the memory of the man shaking him, demanding that he promise to keep her safe. *My teeth nearly rattled in my mouth. Now I won't have any by the time that guy gets through with me.*

Still, he'd be justified. Milo had failed to do the one thing

that mattered most. A nurse appeared with a small glass. "I
have powder for the pain. Are you ready for it?"

"Will it make me sleepy?"

She just smiled and shook her head as she helped him sit
up and drink through a paper straw. "Drink it all. I know it
hurts, but it won't soon."

A couple of minutes later, he realized that shaking head
had been a lie. He'd be out in no time.

DECEMBER NINTH. Clarice set the last nutcracker in the last
crate herself. Mr. Gaines had assured her that the "supplies"
Mr. Topo had provided—supplies he hadn't been allowed to
touch, of course—had been removed the day after Thanksgiving. Mr. Dalton assured her that the men would arrive at eight
o'clock the following evening.

And Milo will be there. Detective Doyle better keep him alive.

With that done, Clarice walked past the painters' corner
and waved at the girls. "We did it! I know some of you pitched
in and helped when you had time. I really appreciate it. I'm
buying lunch today."

A cheer went up, but Edith looked skeptical. "What's
wrong?"

It can't show. I can't show how nervous I am. Then she realized
she could. "So many things to learn. The good thing about
that order was I didn't have to think about all the things I
don't know. Now…"

"You'll do fine. Everyone thought you'd get all high-
falutin' on us, but you didn't. You just kept working." A note
of sincerity entered her tone as she added, "We should have
known better. You weren't that way before—not even when
Meyer showed favoritism."

Not knowing how to respond to that, Clarice just thanked
them and asked that they make a list of what they wanted for

lunch. "I'll send Mr. Dalton after it. He'll enjoy getting out of the office for a few minutes."

Actually, for all she knew, he'd hate that, but Clarice didn't have time to think about it. As she made her way up the stairs, something she'd been pondering for two weeks now finally came together into one more section of the puzzle. She turned at the top of the stairs and ran down as if desperate to get away. There. That was it. That was the difference in the sound.

Once in the office, she told Mr. Dalton about her lunchtime errand and pulled her purse from the shelf next to her office door. From her change purse, she pulled several dollars and took it back to him. "Get a box of doughnuts, will you? Make sure there's yours and Mr. Gaines' favorites in there, too."

"Very kind of you, Miss Stahl, but the petty cash—"

"This is my personal treat, but thanks just the same."

The morning paper still lay folded on the chair next to Mr. Dalton's desk. "Mind if I read that? Uncle Dietrich did every morning at breakfast, apparently. I just found out on the way to work today."

"Of course. It's your paper. I believe he got the Chronicle at home and the Gazette here."

The Gazette—more prone to sensationalism and evasive reporting techniques. Always truthful, but they did offer as many speculations as facts. Still, even knowing that, she couldn't have been prepared for the headline.

DETECTIVE FOUND FLOATING IN LAKE DANUBE. TOPO BLAMED.

Eyes welling with tears, Clarice read the story of Detective Cosmo Lombardi found shot twice through the heart and dumped in the lake.

—

Evidence suggests that he may have been improperly weighted down. Who knows how many others have been dumped by the local mob hit men? While police won't confirm that they suspect Mario Topo and his organization for the murder, intimating there are other equally suspicious groups, the Gazette has information proving that Detective Lombardi was working on the case of murdered toy manufacturer, Dietrich Meyer. The detective and his partner, Eoin Doyle, were looking into Topo's enforcer, Emiliano Natale as prime suspect for the murder.

—

Even more speculation followed, all of it likely as wrong as the first. Not for a second did she believe Detective Lombardi worked for Mario Topo. He'd known the other man. Romano.

"Miss Stahl?"

Clarice folded the newspaper as Mr. Dalton entered the room. "Yes?"

"That call was from Mr. Holmes. You're needed at the house. He'll be here in twenty minutes."

"At the—but lunch!"

"I'll ensure a fine feast, Miss Stahl. It's a kindness you're doing. I'm sure the ladies appreciate it."

How did you get mixed up in something so ugly?

"Shall I show you the few things we need to settle today while you wait?"

They didn't get that far. Just as he'd brought in a small stack of papers for her to look over with him, the telephone rang again. A moment later, he appeared at her side. "It's Mr. Meyer, miss. He'd like to speak to you."

Clarice seated herself at Mr. Dalton's desk and toyed with the earpiece before pulling the receiver closer. "Yes? This is Clarice."

"Hello, cousin! Martin, here. Say, what do you think about having lunch somewhere? I have a business proposition for you."

"A business—lunch? When?"

"Today! I'll buzz over and—"

"No, Martin. I cannot meet with you today or even tomorrow. How about next week?"

Was that—? Had he—? He had! He'd sworn under his breath. "It really needs to be today, dear cousin. What about after closing, then. Dinner? I know a juice joint that—" He broke off. "No, you're not the type, are you? Well, that's fine. Just fine. Keep the family name respectable and all. What about The Chesterfield?"

What is it with that awful place? Everyone wants everything there. I hope I never see it again!

"I really don't think I have time today. Perhaps—"

"Look, Clarice. I don't want to be the overbearing cousin or anything, but you need to meet with me. Name the place. I'll come right now if—"

That would never do! "No, no. I expect to have guests for dinner, but they should go home early. What do you say to dessert and coffee at Uncle Dietrich's house at say nine o'clock? Is that too late for you?"

"Perfect. You're going to love what I have to tell you. Love it, I say!"

Clarice highly doubted that.

TWENTY-FIVE

The enormous library—well, Lily said it was respectable but nothing over-the-top. She ought to know, Milo decided. Regardless, the library pressed in on him as he paced the room, waiting for Clarice to arrive. In the old man's office, the IRS agents, Detective Doyle, Lily, and even Holmes waited. But they'd given him a few minutes alone with her. Just a few. Then it was time to lay out the plans and be sure everyone knew his or her role.

Lily stepped into the room. "Holmes has gone after her. They'll be back shortly. Are you all right?"

"Nervous. I keep praying, but that doesn't seem right. I haven't talked to God since I was a kid. Now I want something, and I'm bugging Him day and night."

"He listens. He cares. He understands more than you think He does."

"Haven't given my confession since confirmation."

She eyed him for a moment before kicking off her shoes and curling up in one of the overstuffed chairs. "Sit. It's rude to stand there like that."

He sat on the ottoman at her feet, hands clasped before

him and studying the carpet pattern as if it held the answers to life's problems. *Maybe it does. How would I know?*

"Will I offend you if I tell you something that may contradict what a priest has told you in the past?"

"No."

When she didn't speak, he looked up at her. In this light, he saw red in those dark strands of hair hanging down to her chin. Odd that he'd never noticed it before. She gave him a smile that might have intrigued him if Clarice hadn't captured his interest and his heart with it.

"Did you know the Bible—God's Word—says you can confess your sins directly to God? Nowhere does it say it has to be to a priest. We can confess to each other, even. That's in James. It even says we can come boldly before God's throne—for mercy. We can. All by ourselves."

"Might hafta do that. I'll be facing death tomorrow. I should square things away with God first."

Lily shifted her legs to the other side of the chair and huffed. "You should do it because it's right, not because you might die."

She had a point.

"Clarice doesn't love you, Milo." If hearing that weren't bad enough, Lily laughed when he couldn't hide his dismay at those words. "She can't, you goof. But she could learn to. I can see it in her. But if you want her to love you, you have to be someone safe to love. That means belonging to God first."

"I'll never be safe, Lily. I'll hafta leave, and she shouldn't hafta go. It's hopeless."

"Giving up before even trying? Quit being a gloomy Gus and think!" She jumped up, ignoring her shoes, and began an argument that belonged in a courtroom.

Her fist pounded the long table in the middle of the room as she insisted that Clarice deserved hell just as much as Detective Lombardi did. He'd have protested, but she turned to face him. "He's dead, by the way. They found him in Lake

Danube. Shackled to boulders, they think, but the shackles must have come undone."

"Solari, then. Topo doesn't use the lake. Solari does. Topo thinks it's too far to travel with a dead fish."

She stopped, turned to face him, and hooked her thumbs into the suspenders she wore. "One more point for our case. Make sure you let the IRS guys know that."

Unsettled about this IRS thing, Milo went to stand before the window and gazed out at the snow-covered ground. At this rate, they'd have a cold, snowy Christmas. *And at best, I'll be in jail.*

His reflection blurred out the background, and he touched the bandage that still covered his cheek. The scars would be horrible, and unless he wanted half of one, the doctor said he'd likely never wear a mustache again. *"I doubt you'll have any facial hair on that side, and what does surface will be patchy."*

"It's probably best that she sees me like this. A reminder of what she escaped."

"Don't be ridiculous." Lily came over and eyed him closely. "Is that blood?"

He touched his bandage before peering closer into the window. "Looks like."

"Maybe you should change it."

"When we're done here." He shot her a look and added, "Don't want her walking in on that." He sighed. "She won't recognize me in a couple of years. Let her have a decent memory instead of nightmares."

"Oh, come on. It can't be that bad."

Milo just smiled. Maybe Lily Barnes needed her illusions as well.

Movement in the other room hinted something might be happening. "Is Holmes back already?"

A glance at the little mantel clock showed they'd been talking far longer than he'd imagined. He needed to say something. "Lily—Miss Barnes—"

"You had it right the first time, chum. Just Lily will work. We're friends now, after all."

"Thanks for the Bible lesson. I'll think about it."

She gazed at him, their eyes meeting in the window's reflection. "There's a guy in the Bible. Felix. He heard what Jesus did and liked it."

"Yeah?"

"Then he did the stupidest thing anyone ever could."

A pang hit Milo's gut. "Wait… Felix. Is that the guy who let them kill Jesus?"

"No. But yes, too. We all did that. No, Felix heard. He believed even. Was 'almost persuaded' to yield to the Gospel —to let Jesus have his soul. But almost isn't enough, Milo. Jesus only accepts wholesale surrender. You remember that."

Voices in the other room grew louder. In the middle of the din, he heard Clarice's. His throat went dry. "Am I all right? Don't look too bad with this thing on?" He touched his face as if she didn't know what he was talking about.

"You're just fine."

The connecting doors slid open. Milo turned to see Clarice standing there in front of the Christmas tree as if a backdrop set up for a stage. "Milo!"

TEN VOICES SPOKE AT ONCE. Clarice wished she knew how to whistle to put a stop to all of it, but her attempts at whistling had been both dismal and snuffed out by Matron. After all, "Young ladies do not whistle like uncouth boys."

She and Milo sat side by side on the little sofa in the great living room. Two of the IRS agents flanked the fireplace. The other two flanked the doorway. Lily Barnes and Detective Doyle sat on the sofa opposite and as far apart as they could get. In Clarice's opinion, however, Detective Doyle didn't seem too pleased about that.

Holmes sat in a chair by an occasional table as if ready to lose himself in a book, but he never quit scanning the room.

After an ineffectual start, and several suggestions, including how Milo would present himself as a trade in good faith, Lily jumped up and addressed the room. "I think that idea needs to be shot down right now."

Clarice wanted to agree, but she didn't think she'd ever convince Milo of the idea. "It could work," she said anyway. "Mr. Topo doesn't know that I know where Milo is. And now that Milo has shown Mr. Lombardi to belong to Mr. Solari instead of loyal to Topo…"

"No." Milo reached over and squeezed Clarice's hand. "If I come, it'll protect you. I need to be there."

"No, you don't." Lily grinned at his obvious pique. "Listen to me. You said something when we were talking earlier. You said that without your bandage, Clarice wouldn't recognize you."

"Yes…"

Now Clarice knew why he insisted on sitting with his undamaged side to her. Poor man. As if she cared about a scar when he'd been such a hero for her! *Now you sound like one of those dizzy "dolls" on the movie screen with their grand, dramatic speeches and gestures.*

Detective Doyle picked up on that. "Hey… that's right. Even without his mustache he isn't very recognizable. With a different haircut and that scar… you could announce his death to Topo tomorrow, and he'd be free."

"Except he's a criminal in his own right," one of the IRS men said.

Lily rolled her eyes and huffed. "You men. You have no imagination. Yes. He worked for a bootlegger. He beat people up. But he never murdered anyone, and he never personally sold any liquor." She turned to face him. "That's right, isn't it?"

"Well, yes, but the guy's right. I—"

"So, you could get a commuted sentence if you were able to help them find more bootleggers, right?"

Clarice didn't know what any of that meant. Her brain said she should, but the realization that Milo hadn't *killed* anyone and that he hadn't been a "giggle water" runner... well, that meant something. Beating people up wasn't right, but it had to have a lesser sentence than murder or bootlegging. Didn't it?

"The lady's got a point, Frank."

Hope welled up within her. Maybe it was possible after all. Maybe he wouldn't go to prison for half his life. Maybe...

"I propose you get authorization for a commuted sentence. If the crimes he's convicted of are, say a ten-year sentence, his is commuted for 'time served' after spending a few months or years helping you take down whatever other outfit you have to work with. Chicago? New York?"

One of the men by the door spoke up. "There's that group working with Pendergast in Kansas City. If we could get him to help us take out that arm, we'd cut off a big supply heading west."

Milo stepped in at this point. "What would I hafta do?" He almost laughed when Lily answered before any of the men could.

"You arrive. Let's face it. With a scar like that and your obvious heritage, hang out in the right places and you'll get noticed. You know how to provoke people. Do it. Then shut them down. You know how to instill fear in anyone. Do it. Someone will notice. They'll get you before that mob boss, and you're in."

A couple of snickers echoed his own. As if it would be that easy. It would work, yes. It would not be that easy. "I'd hafta wait until my face was mostly healed, or it'd hafta be sewn up all over again."

Clarice whimpered. "Isn't there some other way? If he goes to work for some other crime organization, what's to stop the police for arresting him and putting him on trial again anyway? He could put his life at risk only to have this agreement broken by people who don't know any better. He *saved* lives here. He's going to give you information to take down Mr. Topo's and maybe even some of Mr. Solari's organizations. Isn't that enough?"

Milo slipped a hand under hers, laced their fingers together, and said, "No. It isn't. But if they'll get papers drawn up saying if I help take down this Pendergast guy—"

All four IRS men burst out laughing. Even Detective Doyle looked amused. It took a moment for him to realize that they considered "taking down" Pendergast impossible. Still, if he helped deal a blow to the organization, maybe it would be enough. A glance at Lily showed that the girl was already beginning to understand. *You're so young... how do you understand so much so young?*

The man closest to them said, "I'll go make some calls. If we get agreement, you'll have to come into custody now instead of tomorrow."

"Deal." He shot a look at Clarice before adding, "With a couple of stipulations."

The door guy started to protest, but Lily overrode him. "Like what?"

"I get ten minutes with Clarice in the library. Alone. Someone can stand outside each door and try to listen if they want, but I get those ten minutes."

The man nodded. "Can do. What else?"

"We get to write letters."

All four men began shaking their heads even as Detective Doyle said, "Not going to happen. It's a risk to the whole operation."

"They can each write to some place," Lily said. "That place can forward the mail. A fake catalog store at a post office box maybe. He can be trying miracle creams for his scarring or something." When every man kept shaking heads, she laughed. "You are idiots. Don't you see? If he can't keep in touch, he has no reason to do this for you. He's risking his life for you, and you can't figure out how to get a letter to his girl? And I thought I was dealing with professionals."

She might have pushed too hard, but it worked—a little. One of the men, the only one who hadn't said a word thus far, spoke up. "I'll see what we can do."

"Put it in the document," Milo said. He rose. "Now, if I can have those ten minutes, please?"

All four IRS agents and Mr. Holmes followed them down the hall to the study and the library. The silhouette of one man stood in the frosted glass of the pocket doors. Clarice could almost see the other man through the thick-paneled, walnut door to the hall. In less than a minute, another of the men jogged up to stand before the window, arms over his chest and gazing inside.

Milo pulled her out of eyesight of both men with any kind of view. "They'll think we're spooning over here, but 'em link."

She hadn't been this close to him…well, never. Not where she could see him so well. The dark eyes fringed with thick darker lashes. What she wouldn't have given for those lashes. *Silly. They'd look ridiculous with your fair hair.*

"This could take years, kitten. Two… three at least. It takes time for people to trust you. I hafta act like I'm not in a hurry. I also hafta act like I just got over from Italy. No family. I'll make up a story. I'll find the information they need and then I'll come back."

Come back. "To you" was implied there. What could she say to that? What *should* she say? "I can't promise anything about after you return, Milo." His hand brushed her hair from her cheek, and she almost took back those words. "But I can promise to write. And…" Should she say it?

"That's enough. For now." He winked at her, an awkward,

squinty wink. A chuckle followed. "That's not my winking eye, but..."

"I'll be here when you get home. Maybe that's *all* I can give you, but I can give you that. I'll be here. We can try this again. You can come into the factory and smile at me. Wink. I can pretend not to see you."

A gentle knock told them their time was almost up. Milo tipped her chin ever so slightly, and this time, those lips really did touch hers. Clarice smiled as he stepped back. Step by step he backed away. When he reached the library table, he bumped into it and jumped forward, rubbing his backside. "Ouch!"

Even with the unexpected tears that insisted on forming, Clarice giggled.

Milo said something before striding to the door as if desperate to get away. However, once he opened it, he looked back again. "When you were a little girl, did you prefer to play hopscotch or rump jope?"

"Hopscotch, why?"

He never answered her. He just walked away. Whistling.

Rump jope. Oh, dear. When he realizes what he said...

Less than a minute later, arms wrapped around her. Lily. "I—wasn't ready to—say goodbye." Before Lily could respond, Clarice asked, "Do you know Italian?"

A voice behind them said, "I've heard my fair share."

Holmes.

Clarice looked over Lily's shoulder and said, "What does um... "tea ah-mo" mean?

Lily giggled. To their right, Doyle coughed. Holmes? Holmes just smiled.

TWENTY-SIX

W hen the IRS agents and Detective Doyle learned that Martin was coming for a "business meeting" with her, they all refused to leave. They drove their cars away and returned on foot, each man hiding in a different place in the house. Holmes served as butler again and assured her that families forgot that servants could hear everything they said much of the time.

Doyle said that Martin would offer to purchase the factory. It was a profitable company, he knew something about running such places, and few women would want the responsibility. It would stay in the family and also provide a good income. "And he has the resources to do it."

Though Holmes agreed, Clarice caught something else in the man's demeanor. Holmes didn't like this at all. "What's wrong, Holmes?"

"I think we're all forgetting that Mr. Meyer has connections with the Solari family."

They'd assumed that, of course. It fit with everything else, but with that one statement, the entire puzzle shifted. Instead of the motive for Uncle Dietrich's death being one thing,

Clarice saw it as something else. She gasped. "I think that means—"

Holmes held up a hand. "Time to hide. Tell us later." When all the men left the room for their hiding places, Holmes turned to her. "You see it now?"

"This was about money all the time, wasn't it?"

"Just not in the way you thought, but yes."

Their slices of fruitcake and coffee sat at one end of the dining table. Martin came in as genial as any man should be during the Christmas season, kissed her cheek, held her chair, and complimented her on her dress. Her old, cheap dress. She still hadn't had time to find newer, nicer clothes. *People dying have a way of interfering with one's shopping.*

Uh, oh. Miss Sarcasm had returned.

"Oh, Grubby's fruitcake! Delicious! I wonder where she got the rum."

A sick feeling swirled in her gut. What if the IRS men arrested Mrs. Grueber for purchasing illegal liquor? A pointed look from Holmes prompted her to ask, "Holmes, where *did* Mrs. Grueber get the ingredients for fruitcake?"

"There were a couple of bottles in the liquor cabinet before Volstead was passed. She took them to the kitchen for cooking and medicinal purposes. The rest were poured out. Your uncle made sure of it."

"I see."

"I know where to come and raid the cabinets when I'm feeling parched, don't I?" Martin's hearty laughter hinted he might have already tried to quench that thirst. "Now, cousin. I know you're curious about my business proposal, so I'll get right to it. I've had the factory evaluated as to its value and have come to make you an offer for it."

Although she'd expected it, hearing him throw that at her as if the agreement were already made, signed, and sealed rankled. "I wasn't aware I'd planned to sell it."

That loud laugh burst out again. "You're a funny bird.

Listen, you don't want all this hassle, and I've a good head for business." He pulled out a creamy envelope and passed it across to her. "Look that over. Take it to fussy, old Hibbard and get him to do his diligence or whatever those old fusspots do. You'll see it's a good offer. Then you can set about preparing to enter Rockland society, and I'll take over the efficient running of the factory. No more unpleasantness with rough guys, no more numbers to make your head ache, no more noise, dirt, and uncouth girls to bother your head with."

How did you know numbers make my head ache? It was a stupid question. Mr. Dalton.

Without opening the envelope, Clarice slid it to one side and took another bite of the delicious fruitcake. *I hope we don't have to pour out that rum. This would be delicious for Christmas dinner.*

"Aren't you even curious?"

"As you say, I need to have someone with a more legal mind look at it. I probably wouldn't know half of what it said." She took another bite… and another.

Meanwhile, Martin wolfed down his cake, gulped his coffee, winced, and rose. "Well, I'll go then. I really need an answer before noon tomorrow if I'm to get everything squared away in time."

"Noon!" The IRS men had said to agree to almost anything, so she added, "I'll see what Mr. Hibbard can do, but that's awfully quick."

"He'll do it. Never fear. Perhaps I can meet you at the factory, then."

"Telephone first," she warned. "In case I'm not back when you arrive."

Clarice followed him to the front door and bade him goodnight. Just as he reached the bottom of the steps, she called after him, "Martin, are you sure you want to do this? Don't people frown on employers… *fraternizing* with their employees? Especially with ladies?"

She'd expected to trip him up. Instead, Martin turned a

malevolent glare on her and said, "Be prepared to sign that contract tomorrow, Clarice. You don't want to play games you cannot win."

Only when the door had closed and locked did Clarice allow herself to shake. She looked up at Holmes. "How'd I do?"

"Well. Milo would be proud—terrified, but proud."

OF ALL THE things Clarice had ever expected to learn, the nuances of a "take down" would never have been something she'd known existed much less needed to know. Lily had been promised the full story—what of it they could print, anyway. They'd have it before the afternoon edition *and* their extra would contain more details while the other newspapers would be required to put out an extra just to announce the arrest of Mario Topo.

After Mr. Dalton put through the call to Mr. Topo, Clarice sat at his desk and waited for the man to come on the line. "Hello?"

"I am surprised to hear from you. I understood we would meet tonight."

"It needs to be earlier, I'm afraid."

"That will not be—"

"We'll bring whatever you want wherever you want it, but my cousin is pressing me to sign a contract selling him the factory. If I don't have your final agreement that this will be the end of our business dealings, then I'm afraid I'll have to sign that contract and…"

"No!"

Good. She wouldn't have to confess that she knew her cousin worked for Mr. Solari in some way. What that way was, she didn't know. Blackmail? On whose side? Cooperative? Coerced? What the relationship was, they hadn't fully established, but Martin most definitely was in Mr. Solari's "pocket," as the IRS men put it.

"Excuse me, Mr. Topo?"

"You cannot sell to your cousin. Trust me when I say you do not want this."

Perfect. She gave a very gray Mr. Dalton a thumbs-up and repeated a request for a meeting before noon. "The final dolls are loaded onto a truck, and my driver is prepared to drive them for me. I'll ride in the truck as well, if you prefer, although a taxi would—"

"No. No taxi. We'll send you home in one of our cars and trade at the factory later. You bring Holmes to the picnic grounds on the Fairbury road. Do you know it?"

She didn't, but that was the one place the IRS men had insisted they not go—too open. Nowhere for them to hide. "I don't. Mr. Holmes might, but I don't know. Has he ever met you there before?"

The wire went silent except for occasional buzzing and crackling for some time before Mr. Topo returned. "All right. There is an empty warehouse—half burned on Bowman and Grafton. Pull the truck in on the unburned side. We'll be waiting. Eleven o'clock." The line went dead.

"I need to go tell Holmes. Be right back," she informed Mr. Dalton. She hadn't made it to the stairs before she heard him talking low to someone. At the bottom of the stairs, two of the IRS men, dressed in coveralls met her. She told them the meeting place, removed her shoes, and led one of the men back up the stairs. At the entrance to the office door, she took a breath and stepped in just in time to see him pull a gun from the bottom drawer and put it in his coat pocket.

"Going somewhere, Mr. Dalton?" He stuck his hand in the pocket just as she added, "I assume there are bullets in that one?"

The IRS man entered, gun drawn. "Hands in the air."

Dalton was handcuffed and tied to a chair. "We'll be back to get you when this is over, Mr. Dalton," the agent said.

Clarice had one question. "Did you really hate me so much that you sent Mr. Solari's men to kill me?"

"It wasn't like that." The man positively whined with each word. "I didn't want to do it. They *made* me."

Even Lily Barnes had never rolled her eyes so brilliantly, Clarice decided.

"No, really. I lost money in a poker game, they told me the debt was cleared if I'd just let them know the next time Mr. Topo came to the factory, I said I would, and then they found out that he never came. After that, they had me."

"Uncle Dietrich trusted you."

"If I'd known they would kill him…"

Clarice turned to go. "You'd have done exactly what you did. Cowards always do."

With the doors locked, Clarice slipped her shoes back on and hurried down the stairs. "Do we deal with the other issue now or later?"

"Later. When Meyer comes in to sign the contract."

She'd suspected that would be the final decision, but an argument for not giving anyone a chance for escape had been valid. A glance at the big clock over the door told her they had forty-five minutes. "How long will it take us to get there?"

"Twenty minutes. Tops."

At the truck, the man climbed up into the back and wedged himself between crates. The doors closed, and Clarice went for the passenger door. Holmes reached across to help her in and grinned as she slammed the door behind her. "Let's go!"

"We'll stop and fill up the gasoline tank. We need to spend a little time, or it'll be suspicious." Holmes didn't speak again until they'd pulled into a filling station and the attendant had put in every bit of gasoline the tank would take.

"Two-thirty-five, mister." Holmes handed over the money, and Clarice gaped at the cost.

Before she could ask about it, Holmes headed down toward the old Dry Docks area. "Remember, Miss Stahl. You get out, shake hands with Topo. Get him to agree that this is the end of your dealings with him, and get in the car they've brought. We'll handle the rest. Oh, and put your head *down*. If bullets start flying, glass won't keep them from hitting you, but the doors might."

She'd wanted to ask since the previous afternoon, but now she couldn't hold it back anymore. "Is Milo safe?"

"He signed their agreement. He's already on the way to spend a few weeks with some recently arrived immigrants in New York City, and then he'll head to Kansas City."

"Why New York?"

"Because he speaks fluent Italian, but it's been watered down. He can speak English without much of an accent. If they heard him, they'd know. Being with immigrants will help him come up with a good story and help him figure out nuances. Worst case scenario, they'll give him a speech impediment."

They waited for a fire truck to back into the station before moving on again. Clarice ached to ask about the letters, but she didn't know if she wanted to know the answer yet. Holmes pulled a newspaper from his jacket pocket. "Check out that headline."

The Rockland Chronicle had done them proud. EMILIANO NATALE DEAD. SHOT IN FACTORY.

"He can write, by the way. They'll read everything, of course, but he can write."

He can write.

Tension fairly crackled in the air as they pulled into the yard at the old warehouse. The half that had burned had obviously been wooden, but the brick side—a later addition or the original? Clarice didn't know but it looked sturdy.

Three men with odd-looking guns stepped out of shadows. "What are those guns?"

"Tommy guns. Scary things." He reached over, squeezed her arm, and handed her the keys. "Keep it short. Don't antagonize him, get in the car. It'll be over quickly."

"Stay alive, Holmes. I need you."

She approached the three men, only trembling a little, and asked to speak to Mr. Mario Topo. A silhouette filled an open doorway. The man stepped out. Clarice handed him the keys and asked that he inspect the crates as she'd been instructed.

Topo threw the keys to one of the gunmen. "Check it, Sonny." He eyed Clarice. "Martin Meyer wants your company?"

"I don't know why. He has his own business concerns."

"Don't sell it to him. I'll find you a buyer if you want to sell, but do not sell it to him."

If she could only say what she wanted to, but Holmes had warned her. *Don't rile the man.* "I hadn't planned to sell, but if I do, I'll be sure to find someone who loves children and toys and who doesn't do business in illegal contraband." Though she tried to smile, Clarice failed. "I mean no offense, but…"

"None taken. You are stronger than you look. Dietrich would be proud."

"It's clear, boss."

Clarice offered her hand. "We have an agreement, then? You will no longer use Meyer's toys to… *assist* your other business affairs?"

The man reached for her hand, but a bullet rang out before he could take it. Clarice stepped back. Holmes ordered her to drop. She did. The truck wasn't far. Closer than any of the cars. More gunfire followed, so Clarice crawled to the truck and squeezed under. With her hands over her head, she pressed her face to the ground and prayed like she'd never prayed before.

Men shouted. More gunfire blasted, some hitting the truck above her. Was she safe? What if it hit the gas tank? But she stood... no. It was safer under the truck than in open firing range out there. She heard movement over her and remembered the IRS agent. A moment later, the doors flung open, and more gunshots rang out.

Was it an hour? Two? Five minutes? Twenty? At what point she stopped guessing and started praying, Clarice never knew. Only when a gentle hand touched her arm and said, "Let's go home, Miss Stahl," did Clarice stop. She raised her head to meet Holmes' smile. "You did well."

"I—"

"Just a little bit longer, but we have to go. You need to get cleaned up for your meeting with young Martin. Come on."

The tears that threatened dried faster than freshly laundered clothes in the desert. *You can fall apart later. First, Martin.*

IN A NEW SUIT Lily had sent at Holmes' request, Clarice sat at Mr. Dalton's desk. The peppermint bowl still sat there as if determined to be a part of this horrible ordeal, and Clarice decided she never wanted to eat another peppermint again. Mary entered the room just five minutes before noon. "You called for me?"

"I did. We have a guest coming who has made serious accusations against you."

"Accusations? What kind?"

Clarice held out the bowl. "Have a peppermint?"

"Don't mind if I do." She unwrapped it and popped it into her mouth in one swift movement. "Who said something against me? If it's Edith, well—"

Clarice heard footfalls on the steps. Martin was early. The door to Uncle Dietrich's office creaked a bit. Good. Everything was set. How Lily had fit all the sections together so neatly, she didn't understand. She'd just created sections that though they seemed to fit, they didn't quite. When Lily rearranged them, though…

"Good afternoon, cousi—"

Mary turned and gaped. "Martin! What are you doing here?"

After a flicker of horror, and another of annoyance, Martin's entire demeanor shifted to confusion. "Have we been introduced?" After that, a hard look entered his features.

Mary missed the warning. "What's wrong with you?"

"Shut up."

"You can't talk to me like that! Uncle Salvatore will—"

Clarice decided to end the farce. "I think what dear Martin is trying to convey is that he doesn't want me to figure out that you killed Uncle Dietrich."

Everything shifted. Martin bolted from the room. Mary just stared at her. "I didn't. I—but how—but I—"

"You took a peppermint that night when you went in to see him, didn't you? You offered him the chance to work for your uncle… *Salvatore Solari*. He refused. You hit him with the nutcracker. Milo arrived just as you ran down the stairs and nearly knocked me over."

"How—?"

"The footfalls. They were too light for a man, and the heel hit like a woman's shoe." Clarice sighed. "And you knew about that bowl of peppermints when, as far as I know, you'd never been called up to the office."

"Martin was supposed to kill him if he didn't agree, but he told me I had to do it." Mary sobbed now. "I didn't want to, but he said he'd be my boyfriend if I did it for him. And I knew Uncle Sal would be so proud of me for taking down

Topo's puppet." Each word was punctuated with a hiccough or a sniff.

"Did you send the watchman away, or was that Mr. Dalton?"

By the shock on Mary's face, it was obvious the girl hadn't considered that someone could have been there to stop her. *Must have been Mr. Dalton.* Clarice pulled a handkerchief from her pocket and passed it over. "And they just wanted a way to move liquor across the country, too, I suppose."

"It's where the dough is. Heaps of it." Mary stepped back. "Well, I'm going to go now. I don't think I'll be finishing my work for today." A high-pitched giggle followed. "You really should have let Martin buy the factory. Things will get nasty now."

"That's right, Miss Lanzo, but not for Miss Stahl. For you." The head IRS man blocked the door, his heavy badge held out.

Mary's former tears turned into wails that the entire factory probably heard. Clarice walked them to the top of the stairs, and already she could hear the typewriting clacking and dinging behind her. Lily must have had everything she needed to get her story into the evening edition.

Factory workers all stared as Mary and Martin were led away. Clarice nodded at Mr. Grimes and returned to the office. Leaning against the doorjamb, she sighed. "All this for illegal liquor. If people will *murder* for the stuff, I never want to touch a drop."

"People will murder for anything," Lily said around a pencil held between her teeth. "But this does seem one of the most ridiculous things to kill for."

"There's just one thing I still don't understand."

Lily looked up from her notes but said nothing.

"Why did they move Uncle Dietrich's body across town to The Chesterfield?"

After scribbling a few more lines, Lily tucked the pencil

behind her ear and closed her notebook. "That's the simplest explanation of all. By moving Mr. Meyer to The Nutcracker's suite, it threw suspicion onto Topo and his men. That helps Solari's case with the honest cops and helps Solari discover which ones Topo has on the take."

And that's... simple?

EPILOGUE

O*ctober 29, 1929*
      The overhead light burned bright in the office. Drawings of toys, prototypes of toys, finished toys, and even parts of toys littered every surface, including the walls. At the table, Clarice sat with a stack of letters on one side of her, a newspaper on the other. The headline read, WALL STREET TOPPLES.

In her hand, Clarice clutched the most recent letter from Milo. They'd been careful at first—feeling awkward about their personal correspondence being laid bare for the government to read. Clarice wrote of the trials, Mr. Topo's conviction, and how some claimed the corruption had lessened in the city while others said the Russians had just stepped in and kept the liquor flowing. Milo wrote of trying to read the Bible and understand what it said and about how he missed his mother's cooking and his grandmother's bread.

But as months and letters passed, it became easier to share personal details. Milo admitted it was easier to tell her he thought her pretty when writing it on paper than in person. He shared the stories of seeing her help other girls at the factory or the old man outside. Clarice wrote of life in the home, how hard it had been to go from a loving place with her mother to a cold, institutional one, and how she'd finally found a photograph of her mother. *I look just like her*, she'd written.

Milo had replied that her mother must have been beautiful.

Clarice admitted she missed him.

When her hand brushed away tears and her sigh filled the room, Milo cleared his throat. "It's been a tough day."

She jumped up so fast she nearly knocked over the chair. As if a study in opposites, she turned agonizingly slowly to face him. Milo grinned. "We got 'im. Not Pendergast, but Guisto."

"You're…"

"Released." He swallowed hard. "Free."

If he'd hoped she'd fling herself at him—and truth be told, he had—Milo would have been disappointed. He was. But only for a moment. Instead, she took slow, hesitant steps. He swallowed hard and prayed his face wouldn't repel her.

Standing before him, she finally tore her gaze from his and really looked at the strange S-shaped scar. "It's not as bad as I imagined." Clarice cocked her head as if to see it better. "It's really healed? You're all right?"

When her fingers touched his cheek, he closed his eyes and covered her hand with his. "I lived. It doesn't hurt. I just terrify women and children."

Her hand slid up into his hair as she said, "It doesn't terrify me…" She hesitated before asking, "Is it raining?"

He shook his head. "No… I had to do something before I came here."

Clarice stepped back. "You didn't just arrive?"

"A little over an hour or so ago. I went to see a friend of ours first. You weren't the only person I wrote while I was gone."

Her hurt radiated from her and sent his hopes soaring.

He'd been attracted to her before he left—even cared some for her. He'd fallen in love with her through those letters, though. And now she stood before him bothered that he hadn't come to see her first. It had to be a good sign.

"I went to see Mr. Ellison. He maptized be." Milo coughed. "I sound like I have a cold. *Baptized me.*"

"He—? Right now? Tonight?"

For the first time, Milo moved. He reached for one hand... then the other. 'See, here is water; what doth hinder me to be baptized?' Mr. Ellison agreed." Milo tugged her a bit closer. "Of course, it took reminding him about that jailer and a few other times when people were baptized right away, but he did it." When her smile began to form, he slid an arm around her waist. "I wanted to come to you already committed. Washed. Free—in every way. I wanted to give you a reason to trust me."

Clarice laid her head on his shoulder and sighed. "You're here."

"And I get about three more minutes before Holmes appears to rescue your virtue."

She leaned back and gazed into his eyes. "Then you'd better kiss me before it's too late."

DEAR READER

Oh, boy was the research on this one difficult. The worst part is that Southern California has an actual mob museum that I really wanted to go to… but the virus that shall not be named made it next to impossible. When they finally opened, they required masks. I have asthma. I'm just saying.

I took a couple of tiny liberties with this book. First, the word "mob" wasn't in known use before 1927. That means it might have been possible for certain people to be using it, but it wouldn't have been a common word that everyone knew. Since it feels correct for the era and is such a nice, succinct word, I decided to run with it.

Also, both buttons and bulls were slang words for police officers, and some of what I found hinted that both were for uniformed officers. I chose to use "bulls" only for detectives and "buttons" only for all other policemen as a way to differentiate while using slang. Additionally, I found some cases of detectives working in pairs, but other articles and books seemed to imply that detectives often worked alone except when the regular officers just happened to be in the vicinity *or* when they had someone driving them (but that seems to have been in England. What's with their detectives not driving?).

After a fight to get it right, I decided I had to go with what I found and trust the rest. I suspect I got that police procedure wrong as often as I got it right. Things were different then, but I tried.

Then there was the corruption. I hated writing about corrupt police officers, but in some cities like Chicago, the numbers of policemen "on the take" is staggering—over half in some places. It reminded me of the old Tammany machine in New York. Readers of my Madeline series will recognize Lily Barnes and if they think about it, Chief Thomas. I couldn't make either of them corrupt!

Finally, Kansas City. That was the biggest surprise of all. When you look up organized crime in the 1920s, three main places come up first. New York City, Chicago… and Kansas City! I had *no* idea. So, that had to be a thing. Right?

In the end, as much as I strive for strict accuracy with word choice and historical fact, in a few instances I went with what made the most sense or fit the *feel* of the times to keep the reader from being pulled from the story. I hope I can be forgiven that.

ABOUT THE AUTHOR

Chautona Havig lives in an oxymoron, escapes into imaginary worlds that look startlingly similar to ours and writes the stories that emerge. An irrepressible optimist, Chautona sees everything through a kaleidoscope of It's a Wonderful Life sprinkled with fairy tales. Find her on the web and say howdy —if you can remember how to spell her name.

facebook.com/chautonahavig

instagram.com/ChautonaHavig

amazon.com/author/chautonahavig

bookbub.com/authors/chautona-havig

goodreads.com/Chautona

pinterest.com/chautonahavig

ALSO BY CHAUTONA HAVIG

The Independence Islands Series

Christmas on Breakers Point (series prequel)

Dual Power of Convenience (Merriweather Island)

Bookers on the Rocks (Elnora Island)

Flipping Hearts (Hopper Island)

Finding a Memory (Sparrow Island) — Coming 2022

Meddlin' Madeline Mysteries (5 Book Series)

The Hartfield Mysteries (4 Book Series)

Ever After Mysteries

The Last Gasp

The Nutcracker's Suite

The Ransom of Grete — Coming 2022

BOOKS IN THE EVER AFTER MYSTERIES SERIES

The Last Gasp by Chautona Havig

A Giant Murder by Marji Laine

When the Pilot Falls by April Hayman

Murder at the Empire by Cathe Swanson

The Lost Dutchman's Secret by Rebekah Jones

The Nutcracker's Suite by Chautona Havig

Silencing the Siren by Denise L. Barela

Slashed Canvas by Liz Tolsma

SILENCING THE SIREN

A SNEAK PEEK AT THE NEXT EVER AFTER
MYSTERY!

DENISE L. BARELA

ONE

Andrew paced back and forth, tugging at his blond hair. She couldn't be dead. Impossible! He'd just seen Annabel earlier that week! How could she be gone so suddenly?

They'd gone around the island and spent time just sitting on the beach. She had spent the whole time smiling, and seemed so happy. It had been one of his favorite days spent with her. No worries, no interference, and nothing but the love they shared. Even more, it had been the first day for some time that Andrew felt truly carefree. His future had just disintegrated overnight.

Andrew thought back on their final conversation. Her eyes had been bright when she kissed him goodbye and said she couldn't wait for his next visit. But there had been that fidgeting nervousness that had consumed her for those few minutes.

She'd said she had a surprise for him.

What surprise had she been talking about? Surely, this wasn't it.

Something was wrong about the whole situation, but

Andrew couldn't imagine what it could be. How she could be there one day and gone the next. Nothing made sense.

Thoughts rushed through his head, drowning him in grief and misery. But one question forced its way into every thought: how could this have happened?

He would find the answer, although he had no clue where to start. He needed to know what led to her death. Needed to know who killed her and why they picked her as their victim. Did her kind heart make her an easy target? Could it be because of him?

He would solve this… well, mystery! And he'd make sure the criminals were held responsible. Make sure they were brought to justice. It was the least he could do for her. Maybe it would serve as a way to distract himself from the pain of her loss and the void she left behind in his heart.

His Annabel didn't deserve this fate. She deserved the world and everything in it, but he couldn't give it to her now. Anger clashed and rolled with the grief inside him. A war of fire and ice with no clear winner.

He would solve this mystery and would find her killer.

Even if it was the last thing he'd ever do.

They, whoever "they" were, wouldn't get away with it.

Made in the USA
Las Vegas, NV
21 January 2023

66012073R00139